Acclaim D0008862

ALBERT OF ADELAIDE

"If Larry McMurtry had written *Wind in the Willows,* he might have come up with something almost as wonderful and moving as Howard Anderson's ALBERT OF ADELAIDE. This is a novel that defies analysis and summaries. Trust me. Just read it."
—Mary Doria Russell, *New York Times* bestselling author of *The Sparrow* and *Doc*

"One of the most unusual novels of the year—and extraordinarily touching—ALBERT OF ADELAIDE will have readers entranced while they cheer that platypus on."
—*Richmond Times-Dispatch*

"Quick to satisfy with old-fashioned pleasures: action, adventure, fast friends, and unlikely heroes."   —*Publishers Weekly*

"One of the highest compliments a reviewer could inflict on a novel [would] be the sentence 'I have never read anything remotely like this, and I am older than dirt.' Which is a phrase I find that I have to use for Howard Anderson's ALBERT OF ADELAIDE."   —*San Francisco Chronicle*

"Rich in commentary on weighty themes: power, fear, prejudice, and the fluid nature of good and evil. Most of all, Albert is a charming and compelling hero with the strength to honor his convictions while inventing a new life for himself. Readers who enjoy contemporary fiction with shades of social/political commentary will appreciate this.   —*Library Journal*

"Will recall the unnerving allegories of *Watership Down* or *Animal Farm*...ultimately an exploration of the nature of prejudice."

—*Washington Post*

"Trust me. You will love this book and will find yourself reading passages aloud to your loved ones, maybe even to the dog."

—*Hudson Valley News* (NY)

"Required reading...If you've been searching for an old-fashioned Western with a platypus protagonist, wait no more."

—*New York Post*

"Howard L. Anderson's novel is an uproarious introduction to the menagerie of characters living just outside our enclosures."

—*Barnes and Noble Review*

"Clever...Anderson's descriptive writing immerses the reader in the landscape of Australia's harsh, basalt-strewn wild country... Anderson encapsulates our feelings of alienation in a world where we all travel the same landscape, afraid to live—and die—alone."

—*Santa Fe New Mexican*

"[Albert] is a delightful character who discovers he can be more than an object to be stared at in a cage."

—*Kingman Daily Miner* (AZ)

"Totally original, genre-bending...[Howard L. Anderson has] hit a home run his first time up at the plate...one of those delightful and absorbing narratives that can be taken on a number of levels...You won't soon forget the time you spend with ALBERT OF ADELAIDE."

—*Bookloons.com*

"A pleasing adventure through the outback that tackles big themes while celebrating both friendship and independence... Anderson has built a desert world that could be scary for a lone zoo platypus—thankfully, he is never quite alone, and his story will leave readers smiling."

—*BookPage*

"Charming...a touching and enjoyable read."

—FantasyLiterature.com

"This was one of the best books I have read all year. I enjoyed every moment and hope you will pick it up and join Albert on his journey for self and utopia. And you have to love that cover!"

—Pub Writes (Caitieflum.wordpress.com)

Bookseller Praise for

ALBERT OF ADELAIDE

"*Gunfight at the OK Corral* meets *Watership Down* in this unique story of a duck-billed platypus, Albert, who escapes from the Adelaide zoo and heads north, looking for the fabled 'Old Australia,' the land of peace and freedom for animals. The characters are a riot—drunken bandicoots, gun-slinging kangaroos, the dreaded dingoes, and even a Tasmanian devil. This is more fun than you could ever hope for as Albert, shy and unprepared, finds his inner strength, becomes a cool dude—'The Most Wanted Platypus in Old Australia'—and saves the day. This is imagination at its very best! Delightful and delicious!"

—Susan Wasson, Bookworks (Albuquerque, NM)

"I have just finished reading it from cover to cover and *loved* it! The characters are wonderfully described, the country descriptions are accurate, and the personalities of the characters, so fit the animals to which they are attached it's wonderful! I think the book would reach all manner of readers—young and old, fantasy and fiction buffs."

—Beverly Schreck, Barnes and Noble
(Fort Collins, CO)

"Absolutely loved this quirky book that deals with so many themes—loneliness, where do we belong, how much it can hurt to be in the minority, friendship."

—Valerie Welbourn, Fountainhead
Bookstore (Hendersonville, NC)

"The setting was wonderful, Australia still has a Wild West 'outlaw' image. And, like any good western, the villains were perfectly sinister. It felt like Redwall/Brian Jacques for grownups. Plus, I love the cover!"

—Lorna Ruby, Wellesley Books (Wellesley, MA)

"Down Under fantasy meets the wild, wild west. Albert the Platypus escapes from the Adelaide zoo and sets out to find 'home,' the Old Australia. The characters—kangaroos, bandicoots, wallabies, dingoes, and Albert, of course—romp (or waddle, in Albert's case) through a series of colorful adventures—bar fights, shoot-'em-ups, and a grand finale invoking more of a Civil War battlefield than anything you can think of in Australia."

—Joe Wesbook, Bookworks (Albuquerque, NM)

HOWARD L. ANDERSON

TWELVE

NEW YORK BOSTON

Pages 7 and 9: "The Banks of the Reedy Lagoon," traditional Australian
ballad, author unknown.

Twelve
Hachette Book Group
237 Park Avenue
New York, NY 10017

www.HachetteBookGroup.com

Printed in the United States of America

RRD-C

Originally published in hardcover by Twelve.

First trade edition: May 2013
10 9 8 7 6 5 4 3 2 1

Twelve is an imprint of Grand Central Publishing.
The Twelve name and logo are trademarks of Hachette Book Group, Inc.

The Hachette Speakers Bureau provides a wide range of authors for
speaking events. To find out more, go to www.hachettespeakersbureau.com
or call (866) 376-6591.

The publisher is not responsible for websites (or their content) that are
not owned by the publisher.

The Library of Congress has cataloged the hardcover edition as follows:

Anderson, Howard L., 1943-
Albert of Adelaide / Howard L. Anderson. — 1st ed.
p. cm.
ISBN 978-1-4555-0962-1
I. Title.
PS3601.N5437A79 2012
813'.6—dc23
2011045203

ISBN 978-1-4555-0961-4 (pbk.)

It seems fitting to dedicate this book to an Australian soldier I met at a bar many years ago in Sydney. All I can remember about him was that he had a bad bayonet scar from service in Malaya and that he got me hopelessly lost on the New South Wales rail system before he passed out.

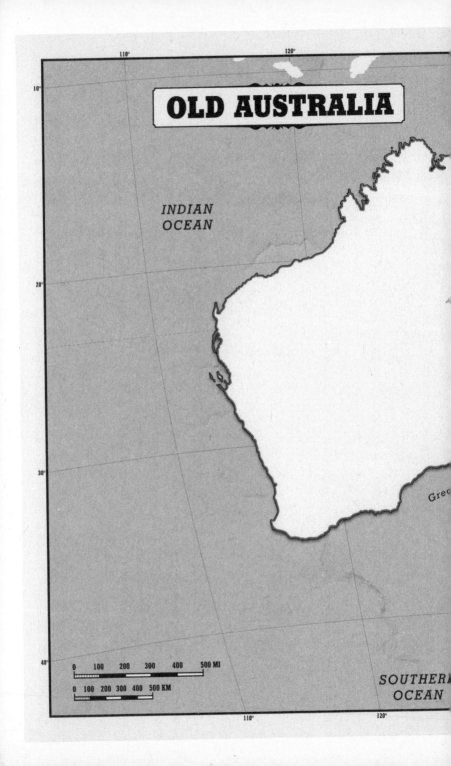

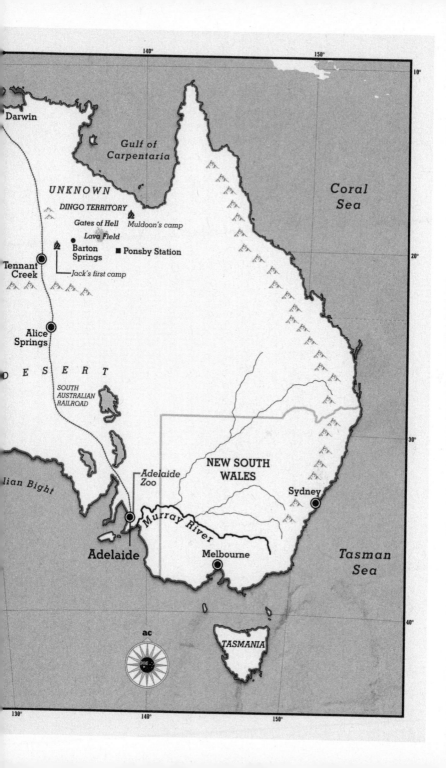

Preface

The county that stretches from Melbourne in the south to Sydney seven hundred and fifty miles up the coast is green with trees and paddocks. On the farms along the coast, sheep graze in the fields, and foxes eat the rabbits that in their turn eat the lettuce growing in the gardens. The sheep, the foxes, and the rabbits live their lives no differently than did their ancestors in England not so many generations ago.

The animals and men that used to live along the coast, in the days before the bush became suburbs, don't come to this part of Australia much anymore. Kangaroos and wallabies have found ways to prosper, but the rest have been pushed back into the deserts or survive in zoos as relics of the past. Tasmanian devils snuffle along the concrete floors of their pens next to panda bears from China. Cassowaries feed in fenced enclosures next to kudus from Africa.

The original inhabitants of Australia have become curiosities to be stared at, along with other unwilling creatures from continents far away. Times have changed along the coast, and there is no room for those that used to live there. The animals living in the zoos remember that Australia once belonged to them.

They talk of a place far away in the desert where things haven't changed and the old life remains as it once was. As with most stories, hope rather than truth wins out with each telling, and in the end the only way to be sure of what's real and what's not real is to go to the source of the tale.

I

Desert Crossing

The tracks of an old railway line run from Adelaide in South Australia to Alice Springs in the Northern Territory. For many years, as each train passed by on its thousand-mile journey between the two towns, passengers threw their empty beer bottles from the windows of the cars into a landscape that seemed unimportant to them. The broken bottles accumulated along the roadbed and the route from Adelaide to Alice Springs became a shining ribbon of broken glass.

At Alice Springs the railway line continues, south to north, in an almost undeviating straight line across the center of the country, and passes through the towns of Tennant Creek and Katherine. The tracks parallel a road that was widened many years ago to take war materials from Alice Springs, in the center of the country, to Darwin on the northern coast. The war drifted away from Darwin to its conclusion in other parts of the Pacific, and traffic along the road slowed to almost nothing. It took almost another lifetime to complete the final nine hundred miles of track from Alice Springs to the coast. North of Alice Springs the railway line disappears into a series of mountain ranges that cross the center of the continent.

Beyond the mountains is a red desert. It is a desert of vast distances and, when closely examined, of great variety. The occasional cliffs and gorges are red in color, as are the soil and sand that cover sections of the desert floor. The color fits well with the blue and normally cloudless sky that on occasion brings water to the dry riverbeds that cut across the land.

The desert is covered in patches of short, stunted grasses that have won a marginal hold in the red, sandy soil. Scattered across the sand and grass, desert grevillea bushes seem like giants in the treeless flats. In some places the bushes grow close to one another, and small birds flutter among the branches. The birds don't sing, and the silence of the desert is broken only briefly by the flutter of their wings.

There are paths in the desert where passing animals have walked the weak grasses into extinction. These tracks, unlike the railroad, follow no set direction. They wander aimlessly through the flats and up and down the banks of the dry rivers, heading to destinations unknown. The age of the tracks is impossible to tell, for the grass grows back slowly in those parts of Australia.

In the early morning of a day long after the war, a small figure walked slowly along one of the winding tracks somewhere to the east of Tennant Creek. On close examination, the figure didn't look any different from most of his kind. He was about two feet tall and covered with short brown fur. He had a short, thick tail that dragged the ground when he walked upright and a ducklike bill where any other animal would have a nose.

The only thing that set Albert apart from any other platypus was that he was carrying an empty soft drink bottle. It was his possession of a bottle, coupled with the fact that he was hundreds of miles north of any running water, that made him different.

Albert had crept away from the railway station at Tennant Creek and into the desert three nights before. For the first day after leaving the station, he had walked along the railroad track. A train had come by late in the afternoon and Albert had hidden himself in a bush near the roadbed. No one had seen him, but he was almost hit by a half-full bottle of Melbourne Bitter thrown from a second-class coach. After that, Albert stayed away from the tracks. From a distance, he had paralleled the roadbed north for the last two days, because without that landmark Albert would have been hopelessly lost. As it was, he was just confused.

The problem was that Albert had no idea where he was going, or exactly what he was looking for. The stories had been vague at best... *somewhere in the desert...a place where old Australia still existed...keep going north...the Promised Land.* Those descriptions had sounded good in Adelaide, but they were worthless in a desert where every direction looked the same.

His escape from Adelaide and the trip to Tennant Creek had been easier than he expected. Security on the smaller animals was minimal. It had been only a matter of time before a careless attendant left his enclosure latch unfastened. Then a quick midnight run through the deserted park and a short swim across the River Torrens had gotten him into the city proper.

Some of the larger animals had been brought to Adelaide by train and then to the zoo by lorry. They told him about the trains and described how to reach the railroad yards. Traffic on the city streets was infrequent late at night, and Albert managed to get across town to the station by hiding behind rubbish bins from the occasional passing automobile. After that, he had hopped a freight to Alice Springs and then another to Tennant Creek, the entire trip courtesy of the South Australia railway.

With the limited resources available to him, Albert had tried to prepare for the journey. He had saved part of his meal at each feeding and put the grubs into a discarded popcorn box he had pulled into his cage when no one was looking. Water he had taken from his dish and put in the stolen soft drink bottle. His planning had gotten him to Alice Springs and then to the desert outside Tennant Creek. Now, he was out of food, out of water, and out of plans.

He had filled his bottle the night he left the train at Tennant Creek, but his bottle didn't hold that much. The water had run out yesterday and Albert knew that if he didn't find more that day, he would die. A platypus is an animal that lives in or near water all its life and can't survive without it. He didn't mind the dying as much as he minded not living long enough to find the place he was looking for, somewhere without people and without zoos.

Albert continued to walk north. He had decided to get as far away from Adelaide as he could before the end. His eyes were red-rimmed from the sun, and his fur was discolored from the reddish dust his feet kicked up as he walked. He had given up trying to make sense of the faint trails that occasionally crossed his path. Albert clutched the empty soft drink bottle and put one webbed foot in front of the other, moving slowly toward the distant horizon.

As the day grew longer, Albert began to hallucinate. Dreams of water would mix with the heat waves rising in the air, and Albert could see the Murray River. He could feel himself slide down the mud ramp in front of his burrow and into the coolness of the river. He would float down the river and watch the green banks pass by. Just when he was sure that he was back for good in the place where he was born, the river would evaporate, and he could see faces smeared with cotton candy and jaws that dribbled popcorn. The faces laughed and handless fingers poked at him through wire mesh. The horror of the visions caused Albert to start shaking, and when he did the faces disappeared. In their place, the emptiness of the desert and the heat of the day would push their way into Albert's consciousness, and he would force himself to begin walking again.

As the day wore on, the brush became thicker and the desert began to give way to bush. Most of the brush was taller than Albert, and he lost sight of the horizon and the railroad track. As the sun changed position in the sky, it became more difficult to tell exactly in which direction he was walking.

After one of the series of hallucinations passed, Albert noticed something in a clump of saltbush a few yards from where he was walking, something with a rectangular outline deep in the thicket of brush. Ignoring the pain from being scratched by the branches, Albert pushed his way into the brush until he came upon a weathered sign that read:

PROPERTY OF THE SOUTH AUSTRALIA RAILWAY
TRESPASSERS WILL BE PROSECUTED

The Management

Just then the wind came up, and Albert knew that it wasn't going to be his day.

He struggled out of the saltbush and once again began walking in the direction he thought was north. The wind blew harder and dust began to swirl around him. Albert shouldered his way through the dust for some distance. He ran into clumps of brush several times and instinct alone told him which direction to take. The dust in the air became thicker, and the world disappeared in a reddish-brown haze. It wasn't long before Albert lost his way completely.

When he realized he might not be going north any longer, he gave up. He was afraid that he might have turned back south, and he didn't want to die any closer to Adelaide than he had to. Albert saw a large desert grevillea through the dust and pushed his way through the wind until he reached it. He crawled under the bush and lay down. The bush blocked a little of the wind and it seemed calmer there. Albert closed his eyes and held his soft drink bottle against his chest. He began laughing because he knew the South Australia railway would never get the chance to prosecute him.

As Albert lay under the bush, red dirt and sand began to drift over him. He began to dream that the sand was the water of the Murray and that he was going home. Above him the wind rattled the branches of the bush.

As the branches rattled, the bush began to sing. The song was very faint. Albert heard "glory," followed by "banks" and then "reedy lagoon." It was a song that Albert had never heard before, and he couldn't understand why a bush would want to sing it to him.

Albert didn't like the song. It took him away from the banks of the river and brought him back to the desert. He wriggled in closer to the roots of the bush and tried to think of home, but the song wouldn't leave him alone.

"I once heard him say he'd wrestled the Famous Muldoon."

Why would a bush listen to anyone? Who was Muldoon and why was he famous? Albert lay there asking himself those questions. The bush couldn't sing very well. It was off-key, and that bothered Albert. It's hard to lie down and die when you are upset. Albert slowly rolled out from under the bush and stood up in the wind. He cocked his head and listened.

And where is the lady I often caressed,
The one with the sad dreamy eyes.
She pillows her head on another man's breast.
He tells her the very same lies.

The song was scattered through the surrounding bushes by the wind. The wind would shift, and with each shift the singing could be heard coming from a different place.

Albert looked out into the dust storm that obscured the desert. He couldn't see more than a few feet, so there was hardly any chance of finding the singer. Yet it was a chance, and one that hadn't been there before. Albert put the bottle under one arm and started walking straight into the wind.

The sand in the air bit into his face and forced him to keep his eyes closed. He pushed on, walking into as many bushes as he walked around. The song flowed out of the wind and washed over Albert like the waters of the river that wasn't there.

High up in the air I can hear the refrain
of the Butcher bird piping his tune.
For spring in her glory has come back again,
to the banks of the reedy lagoon.

With each step the song grew louder. He tried to walk faster. He was sure that around the next bush, or the one after that, he would find where the song was coming from. Just one more verse was all he needed to hear, but the last verse never came.

Albert stopped in front of a large saltbush. He stood for a long time, but all he could hear was the wind and the rustling of the branches. The feeling of hope and his last link with the Murray

River collapsed, and all that remained was the certainty that this was where it would end.

All at once Albert smelled smoke and heard a gruff voice say, "If this is spring in her glory, I can bloody well do without it."

Albert jumped at the sound of the voice. If he hadn't been so tired, he would have run toward it. As it was, he had only enough energy to walk around the saltbush.

There, in the middle of a clearing, with the wind scattering sparks and ashes in all directions, was a small fire. A metal tripod had been placed over the fire, and hanging from the tripod was a battered billycan. Steam was escaping from under the edge of a small plate that covered the top of the can.

On the far side of the clearing, partially obscured by the dust and the flying ashes, a blanket lay spread under a bloodwood tree. The blanket fluttered in the wind and the only thing that kept it from blowing away was the heavy pack resting on it.

Standing over the blanket, with his back toward Albert, was a bulky figure wearing a long drover's coat and a gray slouch hat, trying to tie a dirty piece of canvas between the tree and a salt-bush a few feet away. Each time the creature came close to getting the rope tied, the wind blew the canvas hard enough to pull the rope from his grasp. With each failed attempt, the creature would mutter, "Spring, bah!" and redouble his efforts to tie the canvas to the bush.

After many attempts, he managed to get the canvas tied off so that it formed a barrier against the wind.

The figure in the long coat waited until he was sure the knots would hold the canvas, then nodded in satisfaction and turned back toward the fire. This gave Albert a clear view of him: a large wombat with a graying handlebar mustache.

The wombat, intent on keeping the wind from blowing the

hat off his head, didn't notice Albert watching him from the far side of the clearing.

When the wombat reached the fire he turned his back to the wind, which had shifted and was now coming from Albert's direction. The wombat crouched down and fed small pieces of brush into the fire under the can. As he did, he began to sing in a whooping monotone that carried over the wind.

My bed she would hardly be willing to share
were I camped by the light of the moon . . .

The wombat stopped singing in midverse and began to laugh.

"Ain't that the bloody truth . . . not to mention if I got upwind . . . It's not the keeping square that has kept me single . . . It must be something else . . . I wonder what else it could be . . . I can lie pretty well . . . that can't be it . . . I know it's bathing . . . true love demands soap and water . . . a habit I don't intend to cultivate."

The wombat laughed again and began whistling the song as badly as he'd sung it.

If he hadn't been certain that there was water in the can hanging over the fire, Albert would have crept back into the bush and let someone more desperate than himself confront a singing wombat in a drover's coat.

Instead, he took a deep breath and started to say "Excuse me" in a loud voice. What came out was a garbled hiss. Albert hadn't spoken a word to anyone since his journey began, and he hadn't realized how dry his throat was. The wind had quieted briefly as he tried to talk, so the hissing noise carried clearly to the whistling wombat.

The wombat jumped several feet in the air and at the top of

his lungs screamed, "Snake!" Upon landing, he grabbed a heavy stick that was lying by the fire and began beating the ground all around the spot where he had been crouching. After he finished pummeling every inch of ground within reach of his stick and knocking his firewood all over the clearing, the wombat stopped, looked around, and saw Albert for the first time.

He stared at Albert a few moments, then began to walk toward him. Albert grabbed his soft drink bottle by the neck and prepared to sell his life dearly. Just then the wind rattled a saltbush next to the canvas windbreak. The wombat turned and ran toward the offending bush and at the same time shouted in Albert's direction:

"Thank God, reinforcements. Hurry up and bring your bottle. There's a snake around here, but I've got him on the run."

The wombat reached the bush and began beating it into pieces. Albert was too exhausted to chase a snake of his own making. He walked over to the fire and sat down.

The wombat finished destroying the bush and poked through what was left with the end of his stick. After a careful examination of the debris, the wombat looked over at Albert and said, "Hear anything?"

Albert shook his head. The wombat looked back into the remains of the saltbush and listened for a few moments, then threw down his stick.

"Damn, he got away. That's a snake's luck for you."

The wombat walked back to the fire as if nothing unusual had occurred and lifted the plate off the billycan. He peered inside the can, sniffed it, and put the lid back. "Tea's done. Want some?"

Albert nodded vigorously.

"Got a cup?"

Albert shook his head.

"I sort of figured that, you being naked and all."

Albert wasn't wearing any clothes but he was covered in fur, so as far as he was concerned he wasn't naked. He started to give the wombat a sharp retort, but he remembered what happened the last time he tried to speak. Rather than start the snake business all over again, he kept quiet.

The wombat went over to the pack lying on the blanket and rummaged through it until he found two dented tin cups. He wiped the cups with the sleeve of his coat and brought them back to the fire. He gave one cup to Albert, then filled both cups from the billy.

The wombat motioned to Albert, then went over and sat on the blanket behind the canvas windbreak. Albert got up and sat on the blanket next to him. His earlier fear of the creature had been replaced by gratitude for the tea.

They sat quietly for a while. The heat of the tea passed through the thin sides of the tin cup and burned Albert's paws. Albert ignored the pain and drank. The tea was mostly soggy tea leaves, sand, and ashes, but it was wet and that was enough.

The wombat drank his tea in gulps, ignoring the dirt that blew over him from the gap under the canvas, and stopped only to spit out tea leaves. When he finished his tea, he went over, took the billycan down from the tripod, and brought it back to the blanket. He filled Albert's cup and put the can down next to him, being careful to put the plate back on top to keep some of the dirt out. Then the wombat sat back down on the blanket and pulled out a short-stemmed briar pipe. He proceeded to fill it with tobacco taken from a pouch he pulled from another pocket.

Albert watched and wondered. He had never seen an animal smoke. Then again, he had never seen an animal with clothes on. Maybe, just maybe, he'd reached the place he was looking for. Albert kept thinking as he drank cup after cup of tea.

The wombat didn't say a word. He just smoked his pipe and stared off into the dust storm.

Albert waited until he was sure his throat was wet enough that he wouldn't hiss, then he spoke:

"Is this the place?"

The wombat looked at the pieces of desert being blown around them and took the pipe out of his mouth. "I hope not."

"What I meant was, is this the place where things haven't changed and Australia is like it used to be?"

The wombat thought for a long time before he answered. "If you mean somewhere animals run around without any clothes on while being chased by people with spears and boomerangs, the answer is no. It's not bloody likely that you'd find old Jack in a place like that."

2

Jack the Wombat

The wind had stopped during the night. The sun was high on the horizon, and the coolness of the desert morning was beginning to disappear. The bush that surrounded the camp was silent. The light woke Albert. He pulled the blanket down from his face and squinted at the sunlit tops of the bushes that circled the clearing.

The saltbush was light green against a blue sky, and some of the grevillea bushes sported small yellow flowers that were beginning to attract hoverflies.

The tripod remained standing in the middle of the clearing, a small monument to the fire that had been blown into extinction sometime during the night. The piece of canvas had long since parted company from the saltbush and hung limply from the bloodwood tree. The billycan sat partially covered by a small red sand dune next to where Albert lay.

If it hadn't been for the objects surrounding him, Albert would have been convinced that Jack was just another hallucination brought on by too many miles and too little water. His vague recollection of Jack covering him with a blanket was confused with dreams of being naked and poked with spears.

He couldn't remember very much of what happened after

Jack told him the place he found wasn't the place he expected. Exhaustion had followed hard on the heels of fading hopes.

Albert lay under the blanket for a long time, trying to sort out the night, without much success. The sun rose above the bloodwood tree and dangled the possibilities of a new day over the windblown camp. Finally, Albert sat up and watched several pounds of sand slide off his blanket and onto his feet. He was preparing to stand when Jack started talking in a muffled voice:

"Sardines?"

Albert looked around. "I beg your pardon?"

"I said sardines."

Jack crawled out from beneath a sand-covered blanket. He was still wearing his drover's coat, and his hat was pulled down firmly over his ears. He poked the sand piles that were scattered around the camp until he found the pack.

"I don't know what you eat, but sardines is what we've got."

"Sardines will be fine."

Jack began pulling tins out of his pack. Along with the tinned fish, he pulled out a crushed felt hat and a coat, both articles having seen much wear. Jack tossed the coat and hat to Albert.

"Best put 'um on. It looks like the sun hasn't been treating you too well lately."

Albert reached up and felt his bill. It was blistered and hurt when he touched it. Albert hadn't realized how badly sunburned he had become during his walk north. He'd had other things on his mind.

Albert put on the hat and it fell down over his eyes. He put on the coat, and it felt like a tent had collapsed on him. Albert pushed the hat back on his head so he could see, and rolled up the sleeves, and in a little while he found his front paws.

Jack looked him up and down. "You aren't going to win any

fashion shows, but those should work until we can get something better." He opened two cans of sardines, walked over, and handed one to Albert. "Jack is the name."

"I'm Albert. Pleased to meet you."

Jack sat down next to Albert and began pulling his sardines out of the tin one at a time and eating each one slowly.

"Around the district they call me Jack the Wombat...don't know why. It's not like wombats are thick on the ground. I heard there was a wombat named John east of here...never met him, though."

Albert ate his sardines quickly. He hadn't realized how hungry he was. "I guess that would make me Albert the Platypus."

Jack finished his sardines. After inspecting the tin to make sure he hadn't missed one, he buried it in the sand.

"To tell you the truth, just 'Albert' will probably work. I've never seen or even heard of a platypus, and I've been here a lot of years."

Albert's heart dropped. Not only had he ended up in the wrong Australia, he was ending up as the lone platypus.

"We live in the banks of rivers and don't come out much," said Albert.

"I've never even seen a river," said Jack.

Albert put down the tin of sardines. He wasn't hungry anymore.

"Are you going to eat the rest of your fish?" Jack asked. Albert shook his head, and Jack picked up the tin.

"If you don't mind my asking, what brought you out this way?"

Albert thought quite awhile before he answered the question. "Adelaide."

Jack nodded sagely. "I figured that there was a female behind it."

"Adelaide is a place."

Jack ate a sardine. "Bet you it was named after a female." He smiled as he finished the last sardine and buried the can. "Where are you headed to now, Albert?"

"I haven't thought that far ahead."

Jack started picking up the blankets. "I've got business at Ponsby Station. You can come along if you want."

Albert hesitated. "I'm not sure I belong here."

Jack cocked his head and looked over at Albert. "Maybe not, Albert, but I've walked a hundred miles in every direction, and this is all there is."

If Jack was right, and Albert had no reason to doubt him, staying alone in this desert would be the start of a short trip to the end of the line.

"I guess I'll come with you, Jack...if you don't mind."

"I don't mind. Help me break camp. Get your blanket and grab the tripod." Jack fished a canteen with a shoulder strap out of the pack and tossed it in Albert's direction. "You'd best carry your own water in case you get lost again."

Albert picked up the canteen and put the strap over a shoulder. The canteen reminded him of the soft drink bottle he'd carried into camp. He poked around the sand piles until he found the bottle. He put it in one of the pockets of his coat. The bottle was the only physical evidence of the reality of his journey from Adelaide, and Albert wasn't sure that he wasn't still in the middle of a bad dream.

He took the tripod to Jack, who tied it to the outside of the pack. After a quick look around the clearing, Jack shouldered the pack and set off. Albert followed, trying not to trip over the bottom of his coat.

They walked for several hours, heading north by northeast.

Jack walked at a steady pace, not talking much but occasionally pointing out a plant and telling Albert if it was good to eat or if it had some medicinal properties. Albert was still exhausted from his trip from Adelaide, and it was all he could do just to keep up with Jack, but he kept walking and didn't say a word.

The landscape gradually began to change. The salt and grevillea bushes began to thin, and the red sand gave way to salt pans. The flats were broken only by large rock formations, and in the distance beyond the flats were low hills, and beyond the hills, mountains with gray granite cliffs.

The midday heat finally forced Jack to stop at one of the sandstone formations. There was a shallow cave at the base of the formation that had been scooped out of the soft rock by windblown sand. The cave was on the shady side of the formation. Jack walked into it and put the pack down. Albert followed Jack and sat down at the back of the cave. The sand was still cool from the chill of the previous night and felt good on Albert's feet.

Jack sat for a while, then pulled the tobacco out of his coat and began filling the bowl of his pipe. "I don't like walking in midday. It's best to stay here until the sun starts to go down."

Albert took a drink from his canteen. Jack lit his pipe with a match he struck on the sole of his foot.

"How long were you watching me last night before you came into camp?" Jack asked.

"Not too long," Albert replied. "It was the singing that led me to you."

"I know you saw me singing and talking and making a fool of myself about that snake." Jack looked embarrassed.

"I don't remember much, Jack. I was pretty tired last night."

"I think you remember more than you're saying, and I appreciate it." Jack lit his pipe before continuing. "I've been alone a long time, Albert, and people who live by themselves do silly things because they figure no one else is watching. I try not to make a fool of myself...too proud, I guess...and I hate it when I do."

Albert didn't know quite what to say to Jack, so he didn't say anything.

Jack smoked his pipe for a while, lost in his own thoughts. When he was through, Jack knocked the dottle out of the pipe with his heel and put the pipe back in his pocket. He opened the pack and pulled out a large white rock and an old pepperbox pistol. "Excuse me a second."

He got up and carried the rock outside. He put the rock on the ground, stepped back, and fired a shot at the rock. The noise of the shot bounced off the back of the cave and nearly deafened Albert.

A cloud of smoke and the smell of sulfur drifted into the cave. Jack picked up the rock and examined it closely in the sunlight. He put the rock back on the ground and fired another shot at it. Albert had just enough time to put his paws over his ears before the second shot was fired.

Jack picked up the rock and examined it a second time. He nodded in satisfaction and turned back to the cave. Jack put the pistol in his pocket, and when he did, Albert took his paws off his ears.

"This is a piece of white quartz I picked up two days ago, a pretty rock, but not worth much, unless..." Jack pointed outside the cave. "Take it out in the light and give it a close look."

Albert took the rock into the sunlight outside and examined it closely. "It has gold specks in it."

"It sure does, and those specks make that rock worth quite a bit."

Albert carried the rock back into the cave and gave it back to Jack. "Is it really gold?"

Jack shook his head. "A little bit of it is, but it's mostly iron pyrite, which looks a lot like gold. I take that old pistol and load up two of the barrels with thirty grains of black powder, some wadding, a little gold, and a lot of pyrite, and I shoot it at pieces of quartz. Given a minute or two, I can turn any rock into the mother lode."

"What are you going to do with it?"

"I don't know yet, but I never saw a situation that was made worse by having a little gold."

Jack put the rock and the pistol back in the pack, and pushed the pack to the back wall of the cave. Jack lay down on his back with his head resting on the pack and closed his eyes. Albert had been thinking about what Jack had said about being alone.

"I was only alone once . . . it was after my mother died."

Jack opened one eye. Albert continued:

"When I was young, I wandered too far from our burrow. A dog attacked me and . . . my mother did what she could to defend me. She wasn't very big, but she had a lot of heart . . . In the end a lot of heart wasn't enough."

Jack opened both eyes. "I would have liked your mum."

"I thought she was special, but I guess everyone thinks their mother is special."

After a moment, Jack turned his head and looked at Albert. "What happened to the dog?"

"I don't remember," said Albert.

3

Stones That Speak

They started walking again a few hours before sunset. The temperature had dropped a few degrees, but it was still hot. Jack continued to walk at a steady pace, and Albert found it easier to keep up with him than he had the day before.

Albert had managed a short nap in the cave and felt better than he had in days. He still didn't know where he was going or how he got where he was, but he was moving and that was all that was important. Up until his escape from Adelaide, Albert's life had been one of confinement and regular habits.

His life on the Murray had taken on a dreamlike quality after so many years away from it. Albert remembered those days before his mother died as the good times, a time of warmth and freedom. But in reality the time had been very short, and most of it had been spent in a dark burrow next to the river. He had been protected by his mother and by the earth around him, and had been too young to understand how much more of the world there was.

Albert couldn't remember much of what happened during the time between his mother's death and his capture. Occasionally a memory of that time would thrust itself into his consciousness and the memory would keep him awake for days. The memories were just pictures without sound or movement: a dead dog with his lips curled back over bloody teeth, a cold and empty burrow, a net held in a gloved hand.

In some ways Albert felt his fragmentary recollections of that time, as bad as they were, might be better to have than his memories of the zoo. He remembered every endless day.

They fed him every morning at the same time with grubs and freshwater shrimp. Then he'd be harried down a tunnel from the place where he slept to a caged enclosure with a concrete water tank in the center of it. The tunnel door was shut behind him. Then, he had an hour to wait until the gates of the park opened and the visitors arrived. Albert never saw the gates—they were a long way from his cage—but he always imagined them as sickeningly ornate, replete with images of platypuses being tortured by demons.

There was someone staring at Albert every moment of the fourteen hours a day the zoo was open. He couldn't escape from sight anywhere in the enclosure. They pointed at him, talked about him, made faces at him, and sometimes would throw things at him to make him scramble into the water tank.

The water tank was the worst. There was a glass wall on one side of the tank where people could watch him swim. The glass wall was always clouded by algae growing on it, and the water magnified the faces watching him. Large mouths opened and closed and large eyes blinked ciphered messages to each other behind the blue-green scum on the glass. Albert avoided it as much as he could.

A chill in the air took Albert's thoughts from the Adelaide zoo and brought them back to the desert. As the sun disappeared below the western horizon, a cool breeze began to drift across the trail from the low hills not more than a mile ahead.

Jack pointed toward the hills. "Ponsby Station is on the other side. We'll make camp here tonight…should make the station by noon tomorrow."

Jack picked a likely clearing for their camp and put his pack in the middle of it. As Jack took the billycan and some sardines out of his pack, Albert tried to make himself useful by gathering small sticks to use as firewood.

"Keep an eye out for snakes!" Jack bellowed from where he was putting up the tripod.

"I'll do that, Jack."

Snakes didn't bother Albert. Having his own ability to poison other creatures, he had always felt a certain kinship with them. The venomous spurs on Albert's back legs set him apart from other animals and gave him an understanding of those that used poison to feed or defend themselves.

Albert dropped a pile of sticks next to Jack and went back into the bush to look for more wood. By the time he returned to the camp, Jack had a fire going and the billycan hanging over it.

Twilight was rapidly fading to darkness, and the heat and light from the fire were welcome. Jack opened a couple of cans of sardines, and as soon as the water in the billycan boiled, he poured tea into the tin cups. He and Albert ate the sardines and drank their tea in silence. The night became colder and Albert pulled his coat tightly around him. After Jack finished the last sardine, he stared at the empty tin for a moment before tossing it into the night beyond the campfire.

"Adelaide may have pushed you out into this desert, Albert, but it was claustrophobia that drove me here."

Jack paused to pour more tea into his cup. "I don't know how much you know about wombats, Albert, but we're a boring lot, let me tell you."

"I've seen one or two from a distance, but you're the first one I've ever talked to," Albert replied.

"We live in deep holes, come out in the early morning or late in the evening, eat some leaves, and then call it a day. What kind of life is that? What is there to talk about? Nothing, that's what. Entire conversations consisting of 'What did you do today, Earl?' 'I ate some leaves, Frank. What did you do?' 'I ate some grass and then I slept in a dark hole for twenty-two hours.' 'What are you going to do tomorrow, Frank?' 'I hadn't thought about it, Earl, but I might eat some leaves.' My God, Albert, what kind of life is that?"

Except for all those leaves, the life didn't sound too bad to Albert. "Quiet."

"Damn right it's quiet. It was too damn quiet for me." Jack spit a tea leaf into the fire. "I never could stand the darkness. It made me crazy, and I made my mother and father crazy in return. As soon as I got out of the pouch, I started crawling toward the light. They tried to stop me for a while, embarrassed by what the neighbors would think, I guess. I got bigger and finally they stopped bothering with me. My mother cried occasionally when I'd leave, but that was all. I stayed out all day and at night I'd sleep outside the mouth of the burrow so I could see the stars... Every day I would walk farther and farther from that damn hole in the ground, and one day I walked so far I couldn't find my way back."

Jack stopped talking and stared into the fire.

"How did you get here?" Albert asked.

"I just kept walking and one day here I was. The Famous Muldoon told me once that he thought that everybody who walks far enough eventually ends up here. But Muldoon had strange ideas and I never took much stock in them."

"But where is here?" Albert persisted.

"I can't tell you that, Albert, because I don't know myself. I can tell you that where we are is real and it's a place that can get you killed if you're not careful."

"But what about the other places, the place where everything was like it used to be or the place where those men with the spears and boomerangs live?"

"You hear a lot of stories out here, Albert—some true, some not. Maybe if you'd walked in another direction, you would have found those places. But you didn't."

Jack got up and took the billycan off the hook on the tripod and used the dregs of the tea to douse the fire. "They say that others were here before we were. You can see the drawings they left on the rocks, and those old ones claimed that every bush and every stone had its own spirit."

Albert got his blanket out of the pack and wrapped it around himself. "Do you believe that?"

"I don't hold much stock in those stories...Still, on windy evenings I sometimes think that the stones are singing to me. I just shrug it off, tell myself that I'm getting old and leave it at that."

"What do they say?"

"They don't say anything. It's just the imagination of someone who's been alone in the desert too long."

"What is it that you imagine they say?" Albert insisted.

"They say that there is no point to it all and that everyone that has ever sat on them, crossed by them, or picked them up was coming from nowhere and going to the same place. They giggle a bit and are quiet for a long time. Then they start singing the same song all over again."

"Are you sure it's your imagination? Maybe they are really talking to you."

Jack smiled. "Generally, rocks aren't that intelligent."

He turned away from Albert, walked to the edge of the clearing, and relieved himself on a bush before going to bed.

4

Ponsby Station

The dirt track that led to the center of Ponsby Station went through an old watercourse that had created a shallow gully on the edge of town. Pieces of corrugated tin had been shoved into the sides of the gully at uneven intervals, each piece shading a hole that had been dug into the dirt banks. Ragged flowers in old coffee cans or in pieces of broken crockery graced the shade under some of the protruding tin, and they were the only bits of color in a landscape made up in shades of brown and yellow.

As Jack and Albert walked down the track, Albert could hear an occasional whistle come from one of the holes. "Who lives here?"

"Bandicoots, most likely. They sleep days."

Albert was surprised. "Haven't you been here before?"

Jack shifted the pack to a more comfortable position on his back. "Can't say as I have. It doesn't matter, though. All these places are pretty much the same: bandicoots on one side of town, rock wallabies on the other, all of them working shifts in a half-played-out mine, just trying to get by."

Two hundred yards later, the track opened up into the center of Ponsby Station.

A large ramshackle building stood in the center of a flat piece of ground on the edge of a mining operation. Flattopped hills of mine tailings dwarfed the building, and broken ore carts were scattered along a rusting track leading into the hills beyond the station.

The building at one time had been painted white, but now the walls were nothing but weathered wood with occasional patches of peeling paint. Metal signs advertising beer and tobacco had been nailed up on the ends of the building, but they, too, had weathered, and rusty streaks obscured the painted messages from better times.

The building had a tin roof extending over a long wooden verandah that ran the length of the front wall. A couple of old benches and a spittoon graced the verandah near the front door. The door was closed and the benches were empty.

On the roof was a large sign, also much faded, which read:

PONSBY STATION
GENERAL MERCANTILE
"Quality Goods at a Fair Price"

Sing Sing O'Hanlin, Prop.

Jack stopped in front of the building. He looked up at the sign and smiled. "Here goes nothin', Albert. Stay close."

He climbed up onto the verandah, opened the front door of the mercantile, and walked in. Albert followed him inside.

Inside, the store was not brightly lit. What light there was filtered in from two windows in the back and a dirty skylight over the counter that ran half the length of the store. Behind the counter were shelves of canned goods, bolts of cloth, general hardware, and odd pieces of clothing. A rifle rack holding a rusty flintlock musket and two Enfield carbines sat at one end of the counter. In front of the rifle rack was a glass case containing a few percussion pistols.

The back half of the store was a dirt-floor bar and sporting arena. The bar was two wide planks set across some empty beer barrels. The arena was just an open space with a few wooden bleachers against the wall away from the bar.

A tapped beer keg rested on the planks. The back bar was a long shelf full of whiskey bottles and beer glasses. Above the shelf was a cracked mirror and a series of posters advertising prize-fights that had been fought long ago. Each poster had a picture of a kangaroo wearing shorts on it. The kangaroos had their fists up and appeared to be snarling.

Behind the bar stood a large red kangaroo wearing an apron and a dirty silk shirt with garters on the sleeves. A pair of wire-rimmed spectacles rested on his nose. Across the bar from the kangaroo were two bandicoots wearing canvas overalls. The bandicoots were so drunk they were having trouble standing up.

Jack walked up next to the bandicoots, took off his pack, and set it on the bar. Albert followed him to the bar.

"I assume that's beer in the barrel," Jack said.

The kangaroo looked over his glasses at Jack. "And I assume that there's money in your pocket."

One of the bandicoots snickered. Jack pulled a couple of English shillings out of his coat pocket and put them on the bar. "My money is probably better than your whiskey, but I'm willing to take a chance."

The other bandicoot snickered.

The kangaroo looked at the money and then at Albert. "Are you the only one drinking?"

"I didn't come in here alone. I don't plan to drink alone. Two beers."

The kangaroo shook his head. "I can't serve him," he said, pointing at Albert.

At that point, Albert was much more curious than insulted. Jack's eyes narrowed and he was quiet for a moment before he spoke. "And why would that be?"

The kangaroo gestured to another sign next to the cracked mirror that read:

WE RESERVE THE RIGHT TO REFUSE SERVICE TO ANYONE WHO ISN'T A MARSUPIAL

The Management

"He's going to have to leave. House rules."

Albert spoke for the first time. "I'm a platypus."

The kangaroo adjusted his spectacles with his front paw and took a closer look at Albert. "I never saw anything like you before, and I assume that anything I haven't seen didn't come from a pouch... until proven otherwise."

"Got to be a marsupial," said one bandicoot, nodding his head sagely.

"Marsupial," agreed the other bandicoot.

As both bandicoots and the kangaroo stared at Albert, he could feel the spurs on his hind legs start to extend themselves. The more they stared, the more they reminded Albert of the people at the zoo, and with each look the anger in Albert's soul burned brighter. At the zoo there was nothing he could do, but here he might be allowed the luxury of a violent act. The sound of Jack's voice momentarily halted Albert's downward spiral into rage and the relief of mayhem.

"I say he's a platypus, and you had best leave it at that."

Jack's voice was still calm, but the pepperbox pistol was now sitting on the bar in front of the kangaroo. Both of Jack's paws were resting on the bar next to the pistol.

The kangaroo eyed the pistol a moment before saying, "I suppose I could make an exception in this case. I just use that sign to keep the riffraff out, anyway. What's a platypus?"

The bandicoots, oblivious to what was going on, continued to stare at Albert. "We could look at his private parts," offered one of them.

Albert hit the bandicoot as hard as he could with his front paw. The bandicoot flew across the arena for a few feet before hitting the floor and rolling over to the wooden bleachers. Albert had never hit anyone before and was surprised how satisfying it felt. The spurs in his hind legs began to recede.

The other bandicoot looked over at Albert and said between hiccups, "Good shot, mate. I always thought he was a bit of a poof."

The other bandicoot got up and lurched toward the bar. "Who are you calling a poof?"

The bandicoot in front of Albert put up his fists. "Who was volunteering to look at someone's private parts, Roger?"

"I said *we* could look, Alvin."

"Don't involve me in your nasty plans, you pervert."

At that point Alvin staggered across the room and launched himself at Roger. The bandicoots began rolling around the floor, kicking, biting, and scratching one another.

Jack took the pistol off the bar and put it in his pocket. He watched the bandicoots for a moment, then took another shilling from his pocket and put it on the bar. "A bob on the one with the other one's ear in his mouth."

The kangaroo took a shilling out of a pocket in his apron and laid it on the bar next to Jack's coin. "Done. Your bet's on Roger. He's the meaner of the two. But he gets tired quicker than Alvin."

Jack held out his paw. "Jack's the name."

The kangaroo took Jack's paw and shook it. "Sing Sing O'Hanlin, proprietor and acting captain, Ponsby Station Fusiliers."

"Fusiliers?" Jack let go of O'Hanlin's paw.

"The Fusiliers are our local militia, organized for the defense of Ponsby Station. We meet on Saturdays, march around a little bit, and then we all come over here for a drink. There's good money in those meetings, let me tell you."

Sing Sing took a couple of beer glasses from the back bar, filled them from the keg, and set one in front of Jack and one in front of Albert. "Sorry about any misunderstanding. We don't get many platypuses in here...In fact, you're the first. Have a beer...on the house."

Albert took the beer and thanked Sing Sing, but he didn't feel grateful at all. He was beginning to feel that his escape from the zoo and his flight through the desert had been for nothing. Here he was, where Old Australia was supposed to be, a place where he was to have a home, friends, and others of his kind. Now he was finding that the only way he could even get a beer in this country was at gunpoint.

The bandicoots were beginning to tire. They lay on the floor of the arena and held on to each other by the straps of their overalls, trying to catch their breath. Periodically, one would get up the energy to kick or bite the other, and the scuffle would start all over again.

"Kind of quiet around here," Jack observed, taking a sip of his beer.

O'Hanlin took a glass off the back bar and began to polish it with his apron. "Give it a couple of hours. The wallabies will be getting off shift and the bandicoots will be getting ready to go on. Payday was two days ago, and some of 'um still have money left. They'll get a two-up game going, or maybe a prizefight..."

He looked over at Albert with new appreciation. "Say, this platypus here has a good right hook and..."

"The name's Albert, Albert of Adelaide," said Albert crossly.

Sing Sing didn't miss a beat. "Albert here has a good right hook. We could probably get up a fight that could make us a little money. Nobody here has ever seen a platypus, and they'd figure he'd be easy pickings for one of the local heroes. Might get two... even three-to-one odds."

"I used to fight for money," said Jack. "There's no future in it."

"You a boxer?" asked Sing Sing.

"Wrestled, mostly."

"Boxing is what most people want to see nowadays," said Sing Sing, pointing up at the posters of the boxing kangaroos. "More blood, more action."

Sing Sing picked up another glass to polish and continued, "If the Famous Muldoon hadn't disappeared, maybe people would still be interested in wrestling."

Jack took another drink of beer. "Muldoon could draw a crowd, that's for sure."

"Ever see him fight?" asked O'Hanlin.

"Once or twice," said Jack. "What do you say, Albert, want to make a little money punching the locals?"

Albert had never had a beer before and was beginning to

get light-headed. "I've spent enough of my life having people stare at me."

Jack put his empty beer glass on the bar. "I guess that's a no, Mr. O'Hanlin." Jack picked up his pack and slung it over one shoulder. "Albert and I'll make camp outside of town and come back when things get a little more lively...Have you got a hat and coat that might fit Albert?"

O'Hanlin looked Albert up and down. "Got a vest, anyway. Let's take a look." He walked out from behind the bar and over to the store.

Just then the bandicoots, completely exhausted, quit fighting. They lay on their backs next to each other on the dirt floor.

"I'm sorry, Roger."

"So am I, Alvin."

"Even if you are a poof, Roger, you're the best mate a fellow could have."

"That's right, we're mates."

Roger began to sob uncontrollably. Alvin reached over, patted Roger, and began crying.

O'Hanlin looked at the bandicoots and shook his head. "I should have told you. They do that sometimes."

"It's not a pretty sight," Jack said as he picked up one of the shillings from the bar, "not a pretty sight at all."

5

The Evil Gin Does

As they walked back into Ponsby Station that evening, Albert had much on his mind. He and Jack had set up a camp a few miles out of town. They had spoken very little during the walk to the camp, and even less as they were setting out their gear. Albert guessed that O'Hanlin's reference to the Famous Muldoon was bothering Jack. After all, Jack had told Albert that he knew Muldoon. But, when O'Hanlin mentioned Muldoon to him, Jack had avoided the subject. Albert would have liked to ask Jack more about the Famous Muldoon, but he didn't want to press him on what was obviously a sore subject.

The clothes he had gotten at the mercantile made him feel a little less conspicuous than he had felt wearing the outsized hat and coat Jack had loaned him. O'Hanlin's selection of clothing had been limited, most of the items having been taken in pawn and never claimed. However, after sorting through what was there, Albert, with Jack's help, had selected a fairly clean tweed vest and a much-repaired short canvas jacket with deep side pockets to wear over the vest. Finding a hat had been a little more difficult, but Albert finally settled on a battered kepi with a leather bill. The bill on the hat shaded the bill on Albert's face and he thought it looked rather jaunty in the cracked mirror behind the bar. Jack also found a small rucksack that fit Albert, so they took that also.

Albert had never had to pay for anything before. Life on the Murray had been a matter of digging a burrow and catching lunch in a river that abounded with shrimp and crayfish. The zoo in Adelaide fed its captives with monotonous regularity, but the animals themselves never had to collect the money or buy the food. Now, Albert found that in order to survive he was required to buy clothes and eat canned food; someone had to pay for it.

Jack had paid O'Hanlin for the clothes and the rucksack from a dwindling supply of coins he pulled from a pocket in his drover's coat. Albert tried to broach the subject of how he could pay Jack for the clothes on the walk to the camp, but Jack dismissed Albert's concern by telling him not to worry about the money and that they could work it all out later.

Everything Albert had he had gotten from Jack, with one exception. He still had the soft drink bottle he had brought from Adelaide. When Albert had taken it out of the pocket of his borrowed coat to put in the rucksack, O'Hanlin had noticed the bottle and expressed an interest in it.

It seemed that O'Hanlin, being in the spirits business, was fond of bottles and had a collection of them. He had never seen a bottle like the one Albert had and offered to buy it. Albert had refused to sell the bottle because of its association with his old reality.

However, while he was making camp, Albert began to think about O'Hanlin's offer. Whatever the old reality was, it was gone and a new one had taken its place. The more he thought about it, the more he realized that the less association he had with

Adelaide, the happier he might be. At that point, Albert decided he would sell the bottle to O'Hanlin and give the money to Jack. The money might not be enough to pay Jack what he owed him, but it was a start.

The noise coming from O'Hanlin's place broke Albert's train of thought. He could hear yelling and singing well before they even saw the lights of the building.

The Ponsby Station Mercantile was a much different place at night than it had been that afternoon. Light was streaming through the front windows and the open door. Wallabies and bandicoots congregated in separate groups on the verandah. Some were sitting on the benches talking with one another and occasionally using the spittoon. Others sat on the edge of the porch sharing half-pint bottles of gin or whiskey. The shouting and singing came from inside the building, and every so often a bandicoot or a wallaby would come flying through the open door to land face-first on the verandah. One or two just lay there, more drunk than hurt, and the rest would dust themselves off and rush back inside.

Jack stopped about fifty yards from the front of the building. "Albert, try and keep close to me. Watch my lead, and if trouble starts, get out as quickly as you can. Meet me back at camp, but take a roundabout way back so no one can follow you."

Albert started to get concerned. "What do you think is going to happen?"

"Probably nothing, but you never can tell."

Jack proceeded onto the verandah, followed closely by Albert. He stepped over the fallen and walked through the front door.

The inside of the mercantile was full of smoke and noise. Miners were two-deep at the bar, and O'Hanlin and two assistants were pushing beer and whiskey across the bar as fast as they could. A crowd was gathered over at the arena watching a drunken wallaby throw two coins in the air with a stick. Every time the coins landed, there was much yelling, screaming, and exchanging of money. Every other patron in the bar had a cigar or a pipe in his mouth, and the tobacco smoke hung in heavy layers in the light of the paraffin lamps that lined the walls.

Before they were three feet inside the door, they were stopped by a rough-looking gray kangaroo sitting on a stool by the bar. The kangaroo was heavyset, wearing a bowler hat with a rip in the crown and checked pants with a blackjack hanging out of the back pocket.

"You can go in," the kangaroo said to Jack, "but he's not welcome." He pointed to Albert.

"Why not?" asked Jack.

"Because I say so, and because it's the house rules." The kangaroo stood up and put a paw on the blackjack in his pocket.

"You'd better take that up with your boss," said Jack, pointing to O'Hanlin behind the bar. "Albert here is an exception to the rule."

The bouncer waved his paw toward the bar and caught O'Hanlin's eye. He pointed at Albert, and O'Hanlin motioned for Jack and Albert to come in.

The gray kangaroo sat back down on the stool. "I guess it's all right, but no trouble, you understand? I got my eye on both of you."

"We're no trouble, mate, we're no trouble at all."

Jack pushed on into the crowd. After a few minutes, Jack was able to elbow himself and Albert a place at the bar.

O'Hanlin put a pint of beer in front of Jack and another in front of Albert. "Good evening, Jack. You, too, Albert."

Jack put a couple of coins on the bar and raised his glass.

"Good evening, Mr. O'Hanlin. It looks like you're doing a good trade tonight."

O'Hanlin shrugged. "It'll slow down to a trickle over the next two days. Then nothing until they get paid again in two weeks."

"Mining is a hard life, O'Hanlin; that's why I'd rather find it than dig it up."

"You a prospector?"

Jack nodded and took a sip of beer.

O'Hanlin continued: "Ever make a strike?"

Jack immediately began looking around the room in a nervous manner and put his paw on the bulge in his coat pocket. "What have you heard?"

"I haven't heard anything."

Jack leaned over the bar toward O'Hanlin. "Did you hear that Albert and I have made a big strike?"

"No."

Jack's paw shook as he took another drink of beer. "We'll, it's not true. We haven't found anything, have we, Albert?"

Albert looked quizzically at Jack. "No, Jack, we haven't found anything."

"See, I told you so, O'Hanlin."

O'Hanlin looked suspiciously at Jack for a moment, then broke into a Cheshire cat smile. "Sorry to hear that. Maybe next time."

Jack nodded. "Maybe next time."

O'Hanlin took a bottle of gin off the back bar, poured three shots, and set the brimming shot glasses in front of Jack and Albert. "A drink to Luck, gentlemen, compliments of the house."

Jack, Albert, and O'Hanlin lifted their glasses.

"To Luck," said O'Hanlin.

"To Luck," said Jack, and threw back the shot.

"To Luck," said Albert, and swallowed his drink. It took only a second before he thought he might have poisoned himself. His throat started burning and he felt like choking. Albert immediately grabbed his beer and took a large swallow.

"Gin goes better with a chaser, doesn't it, Albert?" O'Hanlin said, returning the bottle to the back bar.

Albert nodded and took another swallow of beer to wash the taste of juniper berries out of his mouth.

O'Hanlin finished his drink and said, "Take care of yourself, Jack, and don't leave without letting me buy you another drink." He moved down the bar to serve other customers. Jack watched him go and then turned to Albert.

"When a publican like O'Hanlin starts buying you free drinks, you can be sure your luck is going to change, and not for the better, either."

"Why is he doing it, then?" Albert asked.

"Because he's taking the bait, that's why. All you have to do is look guilty and deny everything. It works every time." Jack turned his back to the bar and started watching the game in the arena. Albert turned to watch with him.

"That's a two-up game, Albert. Ever seen one?"

"No."

"See that circle scratched in the dirt?"

"I see it."

"That wallaby with the broken ear over there is acting as the 'boxer.' He's sort of the referee; he makes sure the coins fall in the circle and calls 'heads,' 'tails,' or 'odds.'"

"What's odds?" asked Albert.

"One tail and one head—it doesn't count, and the 'spinner,' the one throwing the coins, has to throw again. If they both come up heads or both tails, then whoever bet heads or tails wins. There is a little more to it, dealing with how many odds the spinner throws before he gets his called coins three times in a row, but that is basically the game."

"It doesn't sound very difficult."

"It was a game invented by alcoholics to amuse drunks; they couldn't afford to make it too complicated," Jack said as he finished his beer. He took a few coins out of his pocket and gave them to Albert. "Stay at the bar for a while, Albert. Buy yourself another drink if you need to. I'm going to wander around the place a little and see if I can find a back door...just in case." Jack winked at Albert and pushed his way back through the crowd.

Jack's place was immediately taken by a large wallaby still covered in grime from his shift in the mine. The wallaby pounded the bar and yelled for beer, until one of O'Hanlin's assistant bartenders slammed a full glass of beer down in front of him. The wallaby threw a coin in the direction of the bartender and took a big drink. The bartender made a signal to the bouncer at the door.

The wallaby took another drink and looked Albert up and down. "What in the hell are you?"

At the zoo, Albert had been an object of curiosity and ridicule. In Old Australia he found himself an object of hate and mistrust. Albert wasn't quite sure how to deal with it, but he was becoming convinced that he had to handle the problem himself rather than passively sitting by and letting Jack stand up for him. "Why do you care?"

"Because, I don't like standing next to some sort of freak."

"Then move away. I was here first."

The wallaby slowly put down his beer. "I'll show you who's going to move!"

Albert made a fist and hoped he really did have a good right hook. Before he could take a swing, he heard a voice saying, "He's a platypus—what's it to you?"

Albert looked down, and there were Roger and Alvin.

"You stay out of this," snarled the wallaby.

"We're not stayin' out of nothin'. Albert here is our mate, isn't he, Roger?" said Alvin.

"He sure is," agreed Roger. "He hit me fair and square this afternoon, and that makes us mates."

"And any mate of Roger's is a mate of mine," said Alvin emphatically.

"You two runts better piss off before you get hurt," said the wallaby.

"Did you hear that, Roger? He told you to piss off," said Alvin.

"But he called you a runt," said Roger.

"You're right, Roger. I'll hit him first."

Just then the bouncer walked up behind the wallaby and hit him in the back of the head with his billy club. The wallaby collapsed on the floor like a puppet with its strings cut. Alvin immediately stepped over to the wallaby's body and began going through his pockets. He found some change and tossed most of it to the bouncer. "Thanks, mate. You can keep the rest."

The kangaroo caught the change in the air, pocketed his club, and started dragging the wallaby toward the front door.

"Never met a wallaby that wasn't a wanker," said Roger, watching the wallaby being thrown through the front door.

"Too right, Roger."

Alvin counted the change he had kept and then ordered three shots of gin from the bartender. "Be a mate, Albert, and hand us that beer off the bar."

Albert took the wallaby's beer and handed it down to Roger and Alvin, who managed to drink all of it before the gin arrived.

Albert was dizzy from the one beer and the shot of gin O'Hanlin had given him, but he couldn't refuse a drink from the bandicoots, not after they had come to his defense. He drank as quickly as he could, but the bad taste lingered. The bandicoots drank their gin almost immediately and started looking in each other's pockets for more money. They couldn't find any.

"Say, Albert, you wouldn't have any quid, would you?" asked Roger hopefully.

Albert took the coins Jack had given him off the bar. He held them down to Roger.

"He's only got three bob," said Roger after counting the coins carefully.

"Not enough," agreed Alvin.

"Not enough for what?" asked Albert.

"Not enough for a proper drunk, of course," said Roger, looking very depressed. "Think of something, Alvin."

Alvin and Roger started thinking. The noise from the two-up game started bothering Albert. The gin was giving him a headache. A lot of shouting came from the arena as the latest spinner made a losing throw. It began to seem like a good idea to Albert to go over and tell the crowd to be quiet. Albert left the bar and walked unsteadily toward the game. Alvin and Roger scampered after him.

Albert got to the center of the little arena just as the broken-eared wallaby started yelling for a new spinner.

"You are making quite a bit of noise," Albert said solemnly.

"Either take the kip or get out of the circle," said the broken-eared wallaby. He held out a wooden paddle and two pennies to Albert.

The crowd had started murmuring the minute Albert walked into the circle. He looked into their faces. "What's the matter, haven't you ever seen a platypus before?"

The crowd started to quiet. Roger and Alvin stepped into the circle beside Albert.

"Well, now you have seen a platypus, and your life is complete. Albert's the name. I'm from Adelaide and I don't give a damn whether you like me or not."

The crowd grew silent. Albert reached over and took the paddle and put the two pennies in the holes in the paddle.

He handed the wallaby his three shillings, and said "Tails" in a loud voice. The wallaby waited, but the crowd said nothing; no one made a side bet. Finally, the wallaby yelled, "No more bets," and nodded to Albert to toss the coins. Albert flipped the coins over his head with the kip. The coins hit the floor inside the circle and rolled to a stop. The wallaby bent over and looked at them.

"Tails."

The wallaby took the coins back to Albert. He put them in the kip and threw them over his head again. Again they both landed tails. The members of the crowd began to make side bets. The wallaby yelled, "No more bets," and Albert threw the coins again. The crowd was quiet until the wallaby examined the coins and yelled, "Tails." As the crowd began yelling, the wallaby took the kip from Albert and gave him two handfuls of coins in return. "You're a winner, mate."

Albert handed Roger and Alvin some of the coins and put the rest in his pocket. Someone in the crowd handed Albert a shot glass full of gin. Albert held the drink up to the crowd. "A platypus is the luckiest animal in the world"—he tossed down the drink and took the kip back from the wallaby—"so you had better bet with me because I am not finished yet."

Albert flung the pennies once again into the air and yelled, "Tails."

The copper coins rose in the smoke-filled air and hung suspended in the flickering light of the paraffin lamps for a fragment of a second before they began their fall back toward the earth.

6

About the Night Before

Albert felt the weight on his chest wiggle a little. He opened his eyes slowly and saw blue sky in a rectangle of rusted steel. The heat surrounding him was oppressive, and he smelled smoke. Albert tried to move his feet, but he couldn't.

He closed his eyes again. He remembered throwing the pennies in the air, the taste of juniper berries, the crowd yelling and pushing, the smell of smoke, and then nothing. Maybe it was a dream—but if it was, why could he still smell the smoke?

Then he heard a voice whispering, "Albert...Albert, wake up. We've got to get out of here."

Albert opened his eyes again. The head of Jack the Wombat had appeared in the blue rectangle. Albert looked around. He was lying on his back in what looked like a rusted metal box with no lid. Albert reached out and put a paw on the side of the box. It was warm to the touch. He looked down at his chest. Alvin, or perhaps it was Roger, was lying on his chest, snoring loudly. The other bandicoot was lying on Albert's feet. Shilling coins were scattered all over the bandicoots and the bottom of the box.

"Albert...get up!" Jack insisted. Before Albert could reply, Jack reached down and grabbed Albert by the collar, hauling him out of the box, and shaking off the bandicoots in the process.

The bandicoots didn't even wake up. They fell into a pile in the corner of the box and continued snoring.

Jack pulled Albert clear of the box, put him on the ground, and crawled back in where the bandicoots were sleeping. Albert looked around and realized that he had been sleeping in the bottom of an abandoned ore cart on one of the tailing dumps above Ponsby Station. It was almost midday, and heat waves were starting to rise from the dumps and the ore cart. Albert couldn't see Ponsby Station, only a column of smoke rising from where the mercantile had been.

Jack climbed back out of the ore cart with two fistfuls of coins. He put the money in his coat pockets. He took a canteen off his shoulder, unscrewed the cap, and handed it to Albert. "It's just water. Take a drink and let's get moving."

Albert took the canteen and started drinking. He hadn't realized how thirsty he was, and just drinking the water began to ease his headache. After drinking most of the contents of the canteen, Albert handed it back to Jack.

"What happened?" he asked.

"I burned down the store. I'll tell you about it later." Jack screwed the cap back on the canteen. "Right now you and I have to put some distance between us and Ponsby Station."

He turned and began sliding down the tailing dump to the desert below. Albert scrambled after him, kicking up plumes of yellow dust in his wake.

At the bottom of the dump, Jack started walking at a rapid pace. "We'd better move east for a while and then circle back to the camp and pick up our gear."

"What about Roger and Alvin?" Albert asked when he caught up with Jack.

"I wouldn't worry about those bandicoots, if I were you. I'm sure they've slept off a hangover in worse places. Besides, I left enough coins in the bottom of that ore cart to keep both of them drunk for a month...assuming they can find a place to drink."

The trip back to the camp was a long, painful struggle. Jack might not have liked to walk in the midday sun, but he made an exception in this case. Between the heat and the gin from the night before, each hour felt like a dozen to Albert. The only water Jack had was in the canteen that he had given Albert, and that was almost empty before the trip started. There was enough water for only a few sips each hour, and Jack rationed it carefully.

Albert was curious about why Jack had burned down Ponsby Station, but he knew that he needed to keep his mind on making it back to camp. It seemed like all he had done since he left Adelaide was walk. None of those walks had been pleasant, but each one had seemed inevitable. Jack was beginning to teach him about the desert, but Albert knew he had a lot more to learn. It was becoming clear to him that he would soon need to strike out on his own.

Old Australia was certainly different from Adelaide. It was not the place Albert had hoped to find. There were places in this desert that the other animals at the zoo in Adelaide had never even dreamed of, and perhaps somewhere beyond the horizon was a place where he would finally find the home that had been lost to him so many years before.

They arrived at the camp north of Ponsby Station a few hours before the sun went down. Jack had Albert wait in the desert a few hundred yards from the camp and went in alone. He returned shortly.

"No one's been there, but I don't know how long that might last." Jack motioned for Albert to follow him, and they walked back down to the camp.

At the camp Jack was all business. After a few minutes' rest and a drink of some much-needed water, he hurried Albert into breaking camp.

"Let's go, Albert. I'll tell you about the fire when we get a little farther down the road." Jack shouldered his pack and started walking west. Albert pulled on his rucksack and staggered after Jack, swearing under his breath to never touch another glass of gin as long as he lived.

Jack finally stopped when it got too dark to see the trail ahead. He led Albert off the trail for some distance before he took off his pack. Albert slipped off the straps to his rucksack and let it fall on the ground behind him. He stood for a few minutes, almost too tired to sit, but finally bent his knees and came to rest on the pack.

"I could use some tea."

Jack shook his head. "Dry camp, Albert. The light of a fire carries a long way at night. It might bring us some unwelcome guests." He took his pipe out of his pocket and looked at it briefly. "Shouldn't even smoke."

He sadly put the pipe back in his pocket and sat down. He fished a couple of tins of sardines out of his pack and tossed one to Albert. "You had a hell of a night."

"I've had a hell of a day, too," replied Albert. He played with the sardine can for a few moments. "What happened last night? I don't remember anything after I started playing two-up."

Jack nodded as he opened his can of fish. "I'm surprised you remember any of it. You and those two bandicoots had a snootful."

"I'll never do that again—you have my word on it." Albert put down the sardine can. "I could use some more water."

Jack got a canteen out of his pack and passed it to Albert. "I wouldn't be too hasty about giving up strong drink if I were you, Albert. Drunk, you're the luckiest two-up player I ever saw."

"I remember yelling something about being lucky." Albert took a drink of water. "I don't feel lucky."

"You should feel very lucky. You won a lot of money and you didn't get lynched," said Jack.

"Lynched? What are you talking about?"

"Are you going to eat those sardines?" Jack asked, pointing at the tin Albert had put down.

"No, and don't change the subject. What lynching?" Albert demanded.

Jack picked up the new tin of fish, but he paused before opening it. "You won too much money and you're different than everyone else. That combination, and the wrong crowd, will almost always guarantee a hanging."

"I didn't do anything wrong...did I?"

Jack opened the sardine can. "No, Albert, you didn't do anything wrong, and that's the sad part about it. If anybody was doing something wrong it was me, but when they saw you flipping those pennies in the air, they forgot all about me."

"I don't understand," Albert interjected.

"When we went into the bar last night, I had that piece of quartz I'd salted with pyrites in my pocket. I figured that I'd let O'Hanlin think he'd gotten me drunk, then I'd flash the rock and let him see those specks of fool's gold, and then, depending on how the play was going, either sell him part interest in my claim for a few quid or sell him a map to the claim. At one time or another I've done both."

"I'd have to guess it didn't work out," Albert thought aloud.

"Too right it didn't work out," snorted Jack. "Nobody cares about a gold mine when a two-up player is on a streak—and let me tell you, Albert, I never saw a streak like that."

Jack separated two sardines that had become stuck together, and he smiled as he ate them individually. "The more I think of it, Albert, the whole evening was a thing of beauty. Too bad you don't remember it."

"Maybe I'm lucky I don't remember it. What about the fire?"

Jack put down his sardines and took the canteen back from Albert. "The fire was a good idea. I just got a little too enthusiastic with the paraffin, that's all."

Jack had a drink from the canteen as Albert tried hard to recall the night before. The last thing he remembered seeing was the coins flashing in the light. He could recall the smell of smoke, but nothing more.

"You were standing in the middle of the circle, winning every toss, and taunting the crowd about being losers with pouches."

Albert sat up straight. "I wouldn't do anything like that!"

Jack smiled. "Face it, Albert, you've got a mean streak."

Albert was aware of the anger that was always floating in and out of his consciousness, and he tried to keep it in check as much as possible. Obviously alcohol had loosened the reins. "What else did I do?"

"I don't recall anything else, but I got kind of busy." Jack continued to sip on the canteen as he talked. "It was clear to me that you were going to win one toss too many, or one of those damn wallabies was eventually going to take exception to being called a loser with a pouch, and when that happened all hell was going to break loose. If we were going to get clear, I figured we were going to need a distraction and we'd need one pretty quickly."

"The fire!" Albert exclaimed.

"Yes, sir, the fire." Jack rubbed his forehead, and Albert noticed for the first time that his eyebrows were missing and his mustache was frizzy and quite a bit shorter than it had been yesterday.

"Is that what happened to your mustache?" Albert asked.

Jack nodded. "When no one was looking I grabbed a tin of paraffin that they had been filling the lamps with and sloshed it in a back corner of the mercantile. I threw some rags on top of the paraffin and then started looking for a match. All I wanted to do was make a small fire with a lot of smoke. After checking my pockets, I discovered I was out of matches and I had to go get one from the front of the store. I must have tipped over the paraffin tin, because when I got back the whole corner of the store smelled like paraffin. I should have known better, but the noise from the two-up game was getting louder, and I figured it was then or never, so I tossed a lit match into the corner." Jack paused for a drink of water.

"What happened next?" Albert insisted.

"Boom, is what happened," Jack replied. "I got blown back almost to the front door. I never saw paraffin act that way, must have been mixed with some naphtha." A wry smile came across Jack's face. "It was the most excitement I've had since Muldoon killed that kangaroo in Winslow."

"Tell me about Muldoon, Jack."

Jack looked at Albert a moment and then looked away. "As I said, I was lying by the front door, and when I sat up I saw the whole back of the mercantile was on fire. The explosion had gotten everyone's attention, and there was a run at the front door. I stood up in time not to get trampled by the crowd, but they pushed me through the door so hard I popped out into the night like a champagne cork."

"And where was I when all this was happening?" Albert was disappointed that Jack wouldn't tell him about the Famous Muldoon, but he was even more disappointed that he had missed an explosion.

"That's what I wanted to know," Jack said. "I thought I might have gotten you killed. I tried to push my way back into the mercantile, but the crowd was pushing too hard the wrong way for me to get back inside. I gave up and ran around to the side of the building. Singed and smoking wallabies and a bandicoot or two were pouring out all the windows of the building, and I knew I didn't have a chance in hell of getting back inside. Then I noticed a trail of shillings heading toward the mine. I figured it had to be you or at least Roger or Alvin, so I followed the trail. I picked up the coins as I went, didn't think it was a good idea to have anyone else tag along. The coins stopped at the edge of the tailing dumps, and it took me the rest of the night and most of the morning to find out where you were. If I hadn't heard snoring coming from that ore cart, I might never have found you."

"I'm glad you found me, Jack. That's another one I owe you."

Jack shook his head. "Nothing good is going to come out of last night, Albert. All said and done, I didn't do you any favors."

"You got me out of Ponsby Station—and like you said, I didn't get lynched," Albert replied.

"Not yet, anyway, but you have to figure that O'Hanlin and some of his bullyboys are out looking for us right now, and I don't think he's the forgiving sort. Even if we manage to give O'Hanlin the slip, the word is going to get around about what happened at Ponsby Station, and you're the one that is going to get the blame."

"That's because I'm a platypus, isn't it, Jack?" Albert said quietly.

"That's the short of it, Albert, and there's not a damn thing either you or I can do about it." Jack stood up and started pacing up and down. "I shouldn't have taken you to Ponsby Station. One thing always leads to another, and the next thing I know something like that fire happens."

Albert let Jack pace for a few moments before he said anything. "You said last night was a thing of beauty."

Jack stopped pacing. "I did?"

"Not more than a few minutes ago."

Jack sat down next to Albert and didn't say anything for a long while. He kept looking out into the desert as if it would give him the answer to some unspoken question. Finally, he turned to Albert and spoke in a low voice.

"Albert, it would be best if I move on by myself in the morning."

Albert wasn't quite sure what to say. "You're the only friend I've ever had, Jack."

"And you're a friend to me, Albert. But I've been here before, and it wasn't a good thing. I hurt the last friend I had more than you can know. Everyone hopes that they can change, me included. It's been eight years now and I haven't changed a damned bit."

Albert had known that sometime he would have to strike out on his own again and keep looking for the place he left Adelaide to find, but he hadn't expected to have to do it so soon.

He had become accustomed to small talk and meals not eaten alone. All that would be gone in the morning, and Albert would miss Jack more than he cared to admit. No matter how he felt, there was no point in making Jack feel guilty. Jack had already done more for him than he had any right to expect.

"It's just as well, Jack. I don't belong here. If I stay, I'll never find the place I'm looking for."

Jack took the pipe out of his pocket again and put it in his mouth without lighting it. "That place probably doesn't exist, Albert."

There was a chance that Jack was right, but it didn't matter to Albert. He had come a long way on a faint hope and would continue on for the same reason.

"It might, and that's enough for me."

Albert and Jack said nothing more that evening. A cool wind came up across the desert, and each star in the night sky cast an infinitesimal amount of light on the two small and silent creatures sitting next to one another in a sea of shadows.

7

Alone Again

The next morning Jack started a fire and boiled water for tea. He kept the fire small, and the minute the water boiled he kicked some sand over the embers. Every so often Jack would look back up the trail they had taken the night before.

"We should be all right for a few hours." Jack threw a pawful of tea leaves in the billycan and after a few minutes poured some tea in Albert's waiting cup.

There wasn't much said that morning. They finished the tea and wiped out the cups with sand. Jack took down the tripod and put it and the billycan back in his pack. He pulled out a few cans of sardines and handed them to Albert. "I know these aren't your favorite, Albert, but you may need them."

He kept rummaging through his pack. "You have enough water?"

Albert shook his canteen and nodded.

Jack pulled out two boxes of matches and tossed them to Albert. "Might need a fire." He continued looking through his pack until he found what he was looking for at the very bottom. He pulled out a small, oilcloth-covered packet and gave it to Albert.

"What's this?"

"It's a Colt pocket pistol. I keep it as a spare."

"I don't know anything about guns, Jack. You should keep it."

Jack shook his head. "This is hard country, Albert. A gun can get you into trouble and sometimes it can get you out of it. I don't know what you're going to find down the road, but it never hurts to go armed. Just pull back the hammer and pull the trigger. The caps are fresh, so it should go off."

Albert took the packet and put it in his rucksack. He didn't really want the gun, but it seemed important to Jack that he have it, and Jack was his friend.

Jack closed his pack and tossed it up onto his shoulders. "Hold out your hat, Albert."

Albert took off his kepi and held it out. Jack reached in the pocket of his drover's coat, pulled out a large handful of coins, and poured them into Albert's hat. "Don't forget your winnings."

Albert shook his head. "I can't take this, Jack. I owe you for everything I have."

Jack shrugged. "I kept enough to keep me going until I sell my rock. Don't flash that money, Albert. I knew a wallaby or two that were killed for less."

Both of them stood there awkwardly for a few seconds, not knowing what to say next. Finally, Albert put his coin-filled hat under one arm and held out his paw. "You've been a good friend, Jack."

Jack looked a little embarrassed as he took Albert's paw and gave it a shake. "I was never one for long good-byes, Albert… I figure to walk back down the trail a little way to see if we were followed, and after that I'm heading as far away as I can get from Ponsby Station. You should do the same."

"Which way should I go?"

Jack scratched his head and thought a moment. "If I knew

where you were going, I might try and give you some advice. But I don't. If what you're looking for is out in that desert, you're the only one who can find it."

"I'll find it, Jack. You can bet on it."

Jack nodded. "You'll do fine."

He turned and began walking back up the trail. After about twenty feet, he looked back over his shoulder. "If you ever meet Muldoon, Albert, tell him I'm sorry."

Jack then increased his stride and moved swiftly away from the campsite.

Albert stood there in the middle of the abandoned campsite and watched Jack become smaller and smaller until he disappeared over the crest of a small rise. He had been alone for most of his life, and the few days he had spent with Jack were the only good memories he'd had since his mother died.

Finally, Albert forced himself into doing the little tasks that all journeys require regardless of their destination. He packed his rucksack with the money and the sardines that Jack had given him. He held back a gold sovereign that caught his attention and put it in the pocket of his coat, along with Jack's pistol.

His pack now contained money, food, Jack's spare blanket, a couple of boxes of strike-anywhere matches, and the soft drink bottle he had carried from Adelaide. Looking at the bottle made Albert realize how far he had come from his days in captivity, and he was glad he'd never gotten the chance to sell it.

A week ago he was, for all intents and purposes, a dead platypus. Now, the zoo was far behind him. He had made friends. He had more food and water than he had when he had left Adelaide, and he was still alive. Each of which was something he had not expected and, when taken together, equaled a small miracle. Cheered by thoughts of his survival, Albert shouldered his rucksack and began walking down the trail away from Jack and what was left of Ponsby Station.

In keeping with what he had learned, Albert walked for a few hours in the coolness of the morning and then found shelter from the midday heat. The county he passed through that morning was similar to that around Ponsby Station: low hills and barren ground. Albert could see another range of mountains far to the east of his position in the hills, and for lack of a better idea he picked the tallest mountain in the range as a point of reference and kept walking toward it.

Albert walked through the late afternoon and into the early evening. The rough trail that had led him from Ponsby Station became more and more faint until he lost sight of it completely in the fading light. He made a cold camp in a depression next to a sandstone outcrop and ate sardines washed down with water from his canteen.

He lay down on his back, using his pack for a pillow, and pulled his blanket over him as the chill of the desert night settled on the sand around him. He looked up at the stars, and for the first time he felt at one with the rocks and sand that had become his home. There was something clean about the desert that reminded him of the river where he had been born. Both the good and the bad were carried by the wind of the desert and currents of the river, and each day brought one or the other or a mixture of both. In doing so, the river and the wind made each day different, and that difference was the salvation of the restless.

Albert remembered what Jack had told him about wombats and their desire to have the same day repeated endlessly. His days in the zoo had been the same endless repetition, and he was beginning to realize that his escape was as much about a need for change as it was to try to find an Australia where he belonged.

The stories of Old Australia had circulated every evening in the zoo, yet none of the other animals had tried to seek it out. In the end they always went back to what they knew—their pens, their cages, and their regular meals.

Perhaps those animals were wiser than Albert. He looked over at the sandstone outcrop and listened very carefully. The rocks were silent and Albert was left without an answer.

8

The Gates of Hell

Albert started walking toward the distant mountain just before dawn. The trail he had been following from Ponsby Station and the country it passed through began to change. Albert found himself picking his way through undulating hills of cracked basalt and saltbush. The ancient lava flow had cooled in folds and then pulled itself apart. In some places the cracks had become deep crevasses, and walking was dangerous.

Morning turned to midmorning, and the heat of the sun began to reflect back from the black basalt. From time to time Albert lost sight of the mountain as he moved carefully through the ups and downs of the lava field. Albert was drinking more water than he intended, and he knew he was soon going to have to find a place to wait out the day.

He moved up a ridge to get another look at the distant mountain, and when he got to the top of the ridge he found himself looking down a gentle slope into the sandy bottom of a large crevasse.

The crevasse formed a narrow canyon that led deeper into the lava. It was shady in the canyon, and the black sand of the canyon floor was easier to walk on than the rough basalt above. The canyon seemed to be heading in the direction of the mountain, so Albert followed it for fifty yards before sitting down. It felt good to sit in the shade with the weight of his rucksack resting against the side wall of the canyon. Albert was cool for the first time since the sun had come up.

He shook his canteen and didn't like the sound of it. His water was getting short, and he had no idea where or when he would find more. He could wait out the sun here in the canyon, but that would mean trying to walk through the lava flow at night, which given the nature of the country could be difficult if not fatal.

He took a drink from the canteen and looked up the canyon walls at the thin ribbon of sky above him. It was like looking into a river; wisps of clouds, like ripples in a current, moved slowly in the direction of the distant mountain. Albert watched the clouds for a few moments and decided that following the clouds down the canyon was as good a plan as any.

All the decisions had been made for him in the zoo, but now he had to make them for himself. The more he made, the easier it became, but it was also becoming obvious to him that some decisions were better than others and that a really bad one could have serious consequences.

Albert stood up, tightened the shoulder straps on his rucksack, and began moving deeper into the canyon. The longer Albert walked, the higher the canyon walls became. The sandy bottom of the canyon would narrow in some places and widen in others. In the wide sections the walls were too far apart to touch with both arms extended. In the narrow sections Albert's rucksack would scrape against them, but there always was enough room for him to squeeze through.

The canyon would veer to the right and then veer back to the left. Several times the canyon bifurcated, and Albert would have to choose which way to go. He would look up at the sky above the canyon walls and try to see which way the clouds were blowing. If he couldn't see clouds, he would take the gold sovereign from his pocket and flip it in the air. Heads he went to the left, tails to the right.

Albert moved through the canyon for most of the day, stopping every so often to rest and take a small drink from his canteen. He knew that he was lost in the canyon, but it didn't bother him very much. After his walk from Tennant Creek, he learned that if you didn't know, or didn't care, where you were going, there was no such thing as being lost. He didn't know where he was when he entered the canyon, and the fact that he didn't know where he was now didn't really change anything. It was cooler in the canyon than it had been on the lava flow, and that was reason enough to be there.

He walked on through the afternoon until the canyon began to darken and deep shadows clung to the walls. The sun was setting somewhere, and Albert knew it was time to start making a camp. He was in a narrow section of the canyon, and he wanted a wider section of the canyon floor on which to lay out his blanket. He began to walk faster, hoping to find a better place to camp before he lost the light.

Suddenly, the canyon opened up into a section that was twenty feet across with side canyons radiating out from it in all directions. It was brighter in the open section. The walls around the opening were not as high as they had been in the rest of the canyon, and they didn't block as much of the fading sunlight. The walls were still too high to climb, but the lower walls gave Albert hope that he was coming to the edge of the lava field.

Albert decided to camp in the opening and deal with which way to go in the morning. The canyon floor was covered in deep sand, which would make a comfortable place to sleep, and if he put his blanket in the middle of the open section, he would be able to see the night sky.

He was in the process of taking out his blanket and a tin of sardines when he glanced up at the canyon wall across from him.

There was a very small, hand-lettered sign painted on the wall of the open space next to one of the side canyons. The uneven surface of the basalt had absorbed the paint in a haphazard fashion, making the sign difficult to read. Albert walked and took a closer look. The sign was a few feet above his head, but even in the dim light he could read it. The sign read "HELL," with a little arrow pointing toward the side canyon.

Albert pondered the sign for a few moments. Any place called Hell was most likely to be unpleasant. Albert didn't really believe in Hell, but one could never be sure.

He could wait where he was until morning. If Hell was really down the canyon, there was no telling what visitors might show up while he was sleeping. Then again, he could immediately head back the way he had come, but there was nothing back there except dashed hopes and some angry kangaroos. Albert knew that whatever future he had lay in front of him, and the most likely path to it was down the little canyon with the sign.

Albert went back to his rucksack and put the blanket and the sardines away. He took out the matches and put them in his coat pocket along with Jack's pistol, then shouldered his rucksack and walked over to the sign pointing the way to Hell.

He moved into the side canyon and almost immediately lost the light. The walls of the little canyon were very close together and curved back and forth. Dusk was beginning to fade to darkness, and the narrow confines of the canyon added to the gloom.

Albert moved as rapidly as he could while he could still see the canyon floor, but soon it was too dark to see even a few feet ahead of him. He extended his arms, and his paws touched the canyon walls. He moved slowly ahead, using his paws to keep himself in the center of the canyon. He tried going as fast as he could, until he stepped off a small ledge on the trail and fell face-first into the sand of the canyon floor. After that he moved much more carefully, extending each foot slowly to gently touch the ground in front of him. He moved forward like that for what seemed like an eternity, until he ran bill-first into solid rock.

He touched his bill to see if he was bleeding, but didn't feel any blood. He struck a match against the rock in front of him. In the flare of the match, Albert saw that he had run into a giant granite boulder that blocked the canyon exit. The boulder had a sign painted on it that said "HELL," with an arrow pointing both to the right and to the left. The match burned Albert's paw, and he dropped it into the sand. He lit another match and, holding it in front of him, squeezed through a narrow gap on the right side of the boulder.

Albert was out of the lava flow and on a rocky plain. He could see several other large boulders in front of him, but the light of the match carried only a few feet, and it was impossible to tell how many boulders might lie ahead of him. When a gust of wind blew out the match, Albert stood quietly for a few minutes and let his eyes adjust to the darkness. There was no moon that night, but the stars were bright enough to give shape to the rocks ahead of him. Based on the shadows, Albert thought that the field of boulders went for some distance. He started making his way slowly forward, when suddenly a rocket shot into the sky from beyond the field of boulders.

The rocket arched high into the night sky and burst into a red ball of fire that lit up the field of boulders for a few seconds before it consumed itself, leaving a few sparks to fall earthward. In the brief flash of red light, Albert could see that all the boulders had the word *HELL* written on them, with arrows that all pointed toward where the rocket had come from.

Albert made his way forward. He went from boulder to boulder in the direction all the arrows were pointing. Another rocket shot into the sky and lit up the boulder field for a second time. After the rocket burned out and Albert's eyes readjusted to the darkness, he could see a faint glow of light coming from where the rocket had begun its ascent.

Albert headed toward the light, which grew brighter and brighter until he rounded a boulder and came to its source. A large one-story wooden building stood at the edge of the boulder field, and a number of lamps hung from its side. Torches had been planted around the front of the building and large canvas signs were hung from poles on the top and at the sides.

The largest sign, lit by paraffin lamps with reflectors, was on the roof of the building. It read "WELCOME TO THE GATES OF HELL." One sign on the side of the building read "WHISKEY AND AMMUNITON"; another read "DRY GOODS." A smaller sign by the front door read "RELIGIOUS MEDALS, MAPS, FEMALES," although someone had taken a paintbrush and crossed out the word *FEMALES* with a couple of rough strokes.

Just as Albert finished reading the signs, a large wallaby smoking a cigar walked out the front door of the building carrying a skyrocket. He wore a white tuxedo jacket and was missing half an ear. The wallaby walked over to a section of pipe that had been pounded into the ground near the front door. He put the rocket in the pipe and lit the fuse with his cigar. Then he stepped back and watched the rocket shoot upward. After the rocket exploded in the sky over the building, the wallaby turned to go back inside. As he turned, he noticed Albert standing by the boulder.

"If you've come for the party, it's inside," he said.

Albert hesitated.

"We have cake," said the wallaby.

Albert wasn't quite sure what cake was, but the wallaby seemed friendly enough. Albert started walking toward the building. The wallaby walked ahead of him and opened the door. When Albert reached the door, the wallaby said, "Welcome to the Gates of Hell—it's our third anniversary," and escorted Albert into the building.

9

Bertram and Theodore

The inside of the Gates of Hell was a large, low-ceilinged room crammed with barrels, boxes, pieces of scratched furniture, dusty bolts of cloth, and piles of things that Albert didn't recognize. The room was as dark as the outside of the building was light, and Albert couldn't see the far wall of the room.

A small table, covered by a dirty checkered tablecloth, and two ladder-back chairs had been placed in the middle of the room. The table and the room were lit by a candle stuck in the neck of a whiskey bottle sitting on the table. Melting wax from the candle had run down the bottle and pooled on the dirty tablecloth.

Sitting in one of the chairs was a ring-tailed possum wearing a cravat and a once-white tuxedo jacket, much like the one worn by the wallaby. The possum was drinking out of a shot glass when Albert and the wallaby walked into the building. The possum looked over at Albert and blinked several times.

The wallaby hurried over to a pile of furniture and started looking through the pile.

"You'll have to excuse the lack of light. Theodore is allergic to light, aren't you, Theodore?"

The possum gave a small nod and took a sip from his glass.

The wallaby pulled another chair from the pile and took it over to the table. He wiped dust off the seat of the chair with a corner of the tablecloth.

"Do sit down. Our other guests aren't here yet, so we have time for a little chat."

Albert took off his rucksack, put it by the chair, and sat down. The wallaby sat down next to him in the empty chair.

"I'm Bertram," the wallaby said, extending a paw.

Albert shook Bertram's paw. "Albert."

"Our pleasure, isn't it, Theodore?"

Theodore didn't say anything. He pushed his now-empty glass in Bertram's direction.

"Could I get you a drink, Albert?"

Jack's warning about publicans offering free drinks flashed through Albert's mind. He took the canteen off his shoulder.

"No, thank you. I have water."

"Well, then, at least let me get you a glass."

Bertram went over to one of the piles lying around the room and extracted a bottle of whiskey and two dirty glasses. He brought them back to the table, where he wiped the glasses with another corner of the tablecloth. He gave one glass to Albert, then filled his and Theodore's glasses from the bottle.

"What brings you to the Gates of Hell, Albert?" Bertram asked.

"I saw some signs pointing this way, and then I saw the rockets," Albert answered as he poured the last of his water into the dirty glass and looped the canteen strap over his shoulder.

Bertram smiled widely. "The power of advertising...As I have said more than once, Theodore and I owe our success to advertising. Don't we, Theodore?"

Theodore nodded.

"We have even considered starting our own newspaper," Bertram continued.

"Why do you call this place the Gates of Hell?" asked Albert.

"Hell is a metaphysical concept that incites curiosity, and curiosity is a key factor in advertising. It brought you here, didn't it?"

After a brief hesitation, Albert responded, "I guess so."

Bertram continued. "We could have called the place the Gates of Heaven, but it would have attracted the wrong sort, and besides, 'Hell' has a much better ring to it, don't you think? Are you sure I can't get you a drink?"

Albert shook his head. He was beginning to get a very bad feeling about Bertram and Theodore. Albert slowly put his paw into the pocket of his jacket.

"I was wondering if I could purchase some water and supplies from you?"

Bertram looked over at Theodore. The possum gave Albert a hard look, then nodded to the wallaby. Bertram turned back to Albert and smiled.

"Actually, we don't sell supplies."

"But the signs outside—"

Before Albert could finish, Bertram interrupted him. "As I said, Theodore and I owe our success to advertising, not to being truthful."

"Then what do you do?" Albert asked, knowing he wasn't going to like the answer.

"We rob people," said Bertram.

Albert looked over and saw that a small pistol had appeared in Theodore's paw.

"It's not that we started out thieves. Originally, we had a

vision of creating a vast mercantile empire, didn't we, Theodore?" Bertram said earnestly.

Theodore nodded. The barrel of the pistol pointing at Albert's stomach remained steady.

"Unfortunately, buying low and selling high is not as easy as it seems," Bertram continued. "It takes time to build a business, and Theodore became impatient."

The possum picked up his glass with his free paw, finished the whiskey in it, and, without ever taking his eyes off Albert, put the glass on the table and pushed it in Bertram's direction.

"Are you sure I can't get you a drink, Albert? I'm afraid I lied about there being cake." Bertram picked up the whiskey bottle and filled Theodore's glass.

Albert shook his head.

"We started a small store in a town quite far from here, and as I said, Theodore became impatient. One thing led to another and we had to leave. But, as someone once said, 'All's well that ends well,' and here we are celebrating the third year in our new business." Bertram lifted his glass in a toast. "To the Gates of Hell."

Albert sat quietly and made no move to pick up his glass. Bertram looked over at Albert, and for the first time his voice had an edge to it.

"It wouldn't be polite not to toast our success, Albert. You should know that Theodore gets very mean when he's been drinking."

Theodore cocked his pistol.

Albert had become convinced that his chances of leaving the Gates of Hell alive were rapidly approaching zero. He wasn't quite sure what to do next. Albert had his paw on the pistol Jack had given him, but he had never fired a gun, and from the looks of it Theodore was not operating under the same handicap. He decided to try to keep Bertram talking, if for no other reason than to delay the inevitable. Albert picked up his glass with his left paw.

"I'm sorry," he said, lifting his glass. "To the Gates of Hell."

Bertram nodded approvingly and took a drink from his glass. Theodore drained his glass and put it back on the table. He gestured toward Albert's pack with his pistol.

"Theodore is impatient to find out whether robbing you was worth our while. Personally, I prefer to linger over the moment." Bertram took another sip from his glass. "You're not the kind of creature we normally rob. In fact, I don't recall ever seeing anything like you before."

"I'm a platypus," Albert said quietly.

"Theodore and I have never heard of a platypus, have we, Theodore?" Bertram looked over at the possum.

Theodore continued to stare at Albert as he pushed his empty glass in Bertram's direction.

"Two strange creatures in as many days, wonders never cease. Perhaps we should put them on display, another attraction for the Gates of Hell." Bertram filled Theodore's glass.

Albert began to feel a black cloud rising from the pit of his stomach. The spurs on his hind legs began to extend themselves. "I don't think that would be a good idea," he said very softly.

Bertram smiled. "And why not?"

"Because a platypus is a magical creature, and shouldn't be made fun of." Albert began to stare back at Theodore.

"Theodore and I don't believe in magic, do we, Theodore?" Bertram continued to smile.

Albert wasn't sure he believed in magic, either, but he was beginning to believe in anger. "You will before the night is through," he said in the same flat tone he had been using since Bertram had suggested putting him on display.

Bertram hesitated for a moment, then bent over and picked up Albert's rucksack and put it on the table. The noise of the pack hitting the table covered the sound of Albert cocking the pistol in his pocket.

Bertram undid the straps on the rucksack and began to look through the contents. The smile on his face broadened as he reached in the pack and pulled out a pawful of coins. He let the coins trickle down onto the table. "I am beginning to believe in magic, Albert. Tell me more."

Albert watched the coins hit the table for a moment and then looked at Bertram. "I can summon demons."

Bertram cocked his head. "A very interesting but doubtful proposition."

Albert shrugged. "All you have to do is say *zoo* three times, very slowly, and I can guarantee that a demon will appear."

Bertram filled Theodore's glass for the last time. "I don't believe in tempting fate, Albert. We have your money, and that is magic enough for me."

Theodore leered at Albert, and then hissed at him. "Zoo."

The possum's voice was high-pitched, and under other circumstances it might have caused Albert some amusement. Theodore drained the glass of whiskey in front of him and started cackling.

"Zoo!" he almost screamed.

Bertram reached out and touched Theodore on the shoulder. "Theodore, I really don't think this is a good idea."

Theodore shook Bertram's paw off his shoulder. Flecks of foam began to form around the corners of Theodore's mouth. Albert knew he was as good as dead. As Theodore started to drool, Albert attempted to pull the pistol out of his pocket. Theodore began to scream *zoo* for the third time, but before he could complete the word a terrible howl came from the darkness in the back of the store.

Theodore swiveled his gun toward the noise. When he did, Albert jerked the pistol free of his pocket and pulled the trigger. The shot missed Theodore, but the muzzle blast blew out the candle. A second before the room went dark, Albert saw a strange creature wearing red underwear and swinging a long chain come running out of the blackness toward Theodore. There was a moment of darkness, then the muzzle flash of Theodore's pistol lit up the room. Albert saw a flash of chain in the light and heard the chain strike flesh. Not knowing what else to do, Albert cocked his pistol and fired another shot where he had last seen Bertram. Before he could fire again, the front door of the Gates of Hell flew open, and Bertram was silhouetted in the doorway for the second it took him to run outside and slam the door behind him.

With the closing of the door, the room reverted to darkness, and Albert was alone with an insane possum and a demon of uncertain origin.

The mere mention of being put on display had started Albert down a road to mindless anger. He had hoped that hearing the word *zoo* would enrage him enough not to feel the pain of being shot and would also release one of the many personal demons that he knew were just below the surface of his being. If anyone tried to torment him, that creature was going to have to pay Albert a blood price.

However, he hadn't expected one of his demons to manifest itself in the form of a creature wearing a set of long johns. Albert sat motionless in his chair and tried to see toward the back of the room. The flash of the pistol shots had temporarily destroyed what little night vision he had. He could smell the stink of black powder in the air but nothing else. Albert knew he had to move from the chair, because whoever was still standing in the Gates of Hell knew exactly where he had been when the shooting started.

Albert slipped off the chair as quietly as he could, but before he could step away from the table, someone called his name.

"Albert!"

The voice was low and had a strange accent. It had to be the demon. Albert pointed his pistol in the direction of the voice.

"Albert, we got enough problems without you pointing a pistol at the only friend you've got within fifty miles."

Albert hesitated.

"We've got to get out of here. Any minute this place is going to be crawling with dingoes. If they didn't hear the shots, you can bet that Bertram will fetch them as fast as he can."

Albert hadn't heard the word *dingo* since he had left the zoo in Adelaide. He had never seen a dingo, but the other animals in the zoo would mention the name only in whispers. It was claimed that they had invaded Old Australia in times long past and that they ate the flesh of other animals. There were some who claimed to have seen them, but the descriptions had been vague, and most of the other animals were convinced that if anyone saw a dingo, he wouldn't live to tell the tale.

Albert didn't know for sure what a dingo was, but he had met Bertram, and given the choice between Bertram and a demon, it was the demon every time. Albert put the pistol back in his pocket. "Where are we going?" he asked.

"As far as we can get before the sun rises."

Albert heard the rattle of the demon's chain and a furry paw took his wrist.

"I can see pretty well in the dark, but not as good as that damned possum." The demon started leading Albert toward the back of the Gates of Hell. The demon stopped for a moment, and Albert heard a rustling sound. The demon thrust a heavy cotton sack in Albert's free paw.

"Carry this," the demon said, and started moving again.

"What happened to Theodore?" Albert asked the demon.

"With any luck I killed him. I didn't hear him breathing when I took his pistol."

The demon pushed open a door at the back of the room and led Albert down a few wooden steps and onto the flats that led away from the Gates of Hell.

10

TJ

The demon released Albert's wrist a few feet beyond the stairs and took back the cotton sack. The torches and the lamps from the front of the building cast a dim and shadowed light for fifty yards beyond where he was standing and, for the first time Albert got a good look at the demon.

He stood just a little taller than Albert, had a pointed nose, pointed ears, and a band of black fur across his eyes. A bushy, striped tail stuck out the back of the ragged red underwear he had on. He had a leather collar around his neck and attached to the collar by a padlock was a section of heavy chain. The demon had looped the chain over one shoulder He held Theodore's pistol in one paw and the cotton sack in the other.

The demon handed Theodore's pistol to Albert. "Hold this," he said and began rummaging through the contents of the cotton sack. He pulled out a crumpled slouch hat with a wide brim, which he immediately put on. A few seconds later he pulled out a pair of dirty moleskin pants, complete with suspenders. The demon put on the pants as quickly as he could, shifting the chain from one shoulder to the other as he pulled up his suspenders.

He took back the pistol from Albert and put it in his pants

pocket. Then he grabbed Albert's paw in his own and gave it a firm shake.

"I'm Terrance James Walcott, fresh off the boat from Frisco, my friends call me TJ, glad to meet you. You take the sack; I'll carry the chain. If you see anything that looks like a dog, shoot it."

Before Albert could reply, TJ let go of Albert's paw and gave him the sack, then started trotting across the desert flats.

Albert ran after him. "I left my pack inside."

TJ kept trotting. "Then kiss it good-bye. No more talking—sound carries a long way in this country."

Whatever light came from the torches of the Gates of Hell was soon behind them, and Albert found himself struggling to keep up with TJ. Albert had slung the sack over one shoulder, allowing his back to take most of the weight, but it was uncomfortable, and with each step he wished he still had his rucksack.

Albert couldn't see TJ clearly, but every so often he could see him outlined against the night sky, or hear a slight *clink* from the chain he was carrying. TJ kept up the pace and could see well enough in the dark to avoid the cracks and ridges that made traveling across the salt pans dangerous. Albert stayed close behind him.

Running was not something Albert was built for. He was good at swimming, but so far there had been little call for that. He had run from the zoo, he and Jack had run from Ponsby Station, and now he was running from the Gates of Hell.

Even though Albert didn't like running very much, he understood it was necessary. He had now walked into trouble on two occasions and managed to run his way out of both of them. It was true that walking was easier on his webbed feet. But running had proved better for his health. Maybe if he had run that day on the Murray, he wouldn't have ended up in a cage. Albert had just finished the thought when he ran into TJ's back.

Before he could say anything, TJ grabbed his bill and pushed him down into a shallow depression on the desert floor. TJ quickly got down beside him and let go of his bill. Albert stuck his head over the edge of the depression and looked out across the flats. He couldn't see anything, but the light wind blowing across the depression carried the smell of something that he hadn't wanted to ever smell again—the stench of dog.

Pictures of his mother's death started flashing through his mind, and Albert felt himself beginning to shake. The combination of fear and rage that the smell had triggered was difficult to control. One part of Albert wanted to run as far and as fast as he could, just to get away from the smell and the memories it brought with it. Another part wanted to attack something, anything. The spurs on his back legs began to leak their poison onto the alkali where he was lying.

TJ put his paw on Albert's shoulder and pushed him deeper into the depression.

The smell got stronger, and Albert could hear the soft shuffle of many paws on the desert floor. The nearness of the danger had a calming effect on Albert. The shaking stopped. He quietly reached into his pocket, pulled out Jack's pistol, and rested it on the lip of the depression. Without raising his head, Albert pushed himself forward a few inches up the slope of the depression where he could see across the desert.

Sixty yards from where he and TJ were lying, five figures moved across the desert silhouetted against the stars. They had pointed ears and pointed muzzles, and two of the figures had rifles slung over their shoulders. It was too dark to tell if the rest were armed. They were moving in the direction of the Gates of Hell. The group kept in single file and trotted past Albert and TJ's position without looking to the left or the right.

The sound of their footsteps receded into the darkness, but it was a good ten minutes before TJ took his paw off Albert's shoulder.

"If the wind had shifted, we'd have been dead meat," TJ said very quietly as he sat up.

"Were those dingoes?" Albert asked. "They smelled like dogs."

"Not a dime's worth of difference between the two, as far as I can tell. Let's get moving. I don't want to be caught in the open when it gets light."

TJ got to his feet, adjusted the chain hanging from his shoulder, and started moving away from the depression at a slow trot. Albert put his pistol back in his pocket and slung the cotton sack over his shoulder. The contents of the sack were lumpy and dug into his back, but after his glimpse of the dingoes, Albert knew that the loss of his rucksack was a small price to pay for his escape.

They traveled across the flats for most of the night. Several times Albert started to ask TJ for a moment's rest and to see if there might be water in the sack he was carrying, but TJ didn't seem inclined to stop, and Albert kept quiet.

Since his capture those many years ago, Albert had been a solitary creature, and except for the keepers who brought his food, and occasional conversations with other animals, he had depended only on himself. His journey from Adelaide had toughened him physically and mentally more than he realized, but it had also made him realize how dependent he had become on others. If he hadn't found Jack, he would have died on the edge of Old Australia. Now he was depending on TJ, someone he had just met, to lead him to safety. Albert had become obligated to others, and with that obligation had come a connection that he had never felt before.

He knew he had been given the help freely, but he still felt he owed something in return. The debt linked him to Jack and to TJ, and maybe even to some creature he had yet to meet. Albert hoped he would be able to pay his debt when the time came. In the meantime, thirsty or not, he would just keep walking.

Dawn found them at the base of reddish sandstone cliffs that formed the eastern edge of the salt flats. To the north, Albert could see the mountain that had been his destination for the last three days. It was closer now, but still many days' journey from the cliffs.

"Another half an hour and we can call it a night." TJ spoke for the first time since they had seen the dingoes on the flats.

He led Albert up a faint trail that started on the desert floor and continued gradually up the cliff wall. Faded images of animals, snakes, and the handprints of men marked the cliff wall along the trail.

In the light of early morning Albert could get a good look at TJ as he walked ahead of him. TJ was tired, and he stumbled occasionally on the loose stones that covered the trail. The chain that TJ was carrying had rubbed a hole through the shoulder of his underwear, and the skin under the hole was seeping blood. Albert could see powder burns and a gash along TJ's neck just above the collar, and assumed that the wound came from the shot Theodore fired just before TJ hit him with the chain. Watching TJ struggle up the trail made Albert feel a little ashamed for even thinking about asking to stop for rest or water on their trek across the flats.

The trail turned up an opening in the cliff and disappeared over a rise between sandstone walls. The path was steeper, and both Albert and TJ found themselves slipping on the loose rocks and having to use their free front paws to catch themselves from falling face-first on the trail. Albert began to think he wouldn't make it to the top of the rise without stopping to catch his breath. Then he smelled it. He smelled water—and not just a little water, a lot of water.

Albert lunged forward and caught up with TJ just as he reached the top of the rise. Below him the trail led down into a small valley surrounded by the cliff walls. In the middle of the valley was a large water hole with clumps of reeds growing along its far bank. Ghost gums and bottlebrush grew in abundance in the valley, and the morning sun shining through the fronds of two red cabbage palms cast shadows across the water hole. In the brush, a few yards from the water's edge, someone had built a lean-to out of a piece of canvas and tree branches. The blackened remains of a fire lay in a circle of rocks in front of the makeshift camp.

If it hadn't been for the signs of habitation, Albert would have run down the trail as fast as he could and thrown himself into the water hole. But the time he had spent in Old Australia had taught him caution. He waited to see how TJ would approach the campsite.

TJ took a couple of deep breaths and walked down the trail, not stopping until he reached the lean-to. He sat down next to the fire pit and dropped the chain in the dirt next to him. He took off his hat and wiped his forehead with his sleeve. He put his hat on the ground next to him, then pulled Theodore's pistol out of his pocket and put it on the hat. TJ motioned to Albert, who had followed him to the camp. "Albert, I need the sack."

Albert took the cotton sack over to where TJ was sitting and put it down next to the chain. TJ rooted through the sack and after a few minutes pulled out a large pocketknife. He opened the knife, put the blade inside the leather collar around his neck, and started sawing at the leather. "I would have done this last night, except there wasn't any time."

"Can I help?" Albert asked.

TJ stopped sawing on the collar. "Are you any better with a knife than you are with a pistol?"

Albert shook his head.

TJ started sawing on the collar again. "Then I'd better do this myself. I didn't come all the way from California to get my throat cut by a platypus."

The leather on the collar was thick, and it took TJ a few minutes to saw through it. When he finished, he took off the collar and put it down along with the chain. Without another word TJ crawled under the lean-to and lay down. He closed his eyes and immediately fell asleep. Albert had a thousand questions for TJ, but it didn't look like they were going to be answered anytime soon.

He walked over to the edge of the water hole and looked into the water. It had been over twenty-four hours since he had slept and eight hours since he'd had a drink. He was tired and very thirsty, but he couldn't will himself to lean over and touch the water.

When he had seen the water hole from the rise coming into the valley, all he wanted to do was embrace it, to let the water envelop him and carry him back to those days when he was young and his whole world was fifty yards of riverbank. Those days had ended in tragedy, but the instinct of a thousand generations of his kind pushed through his thoughts and fears, demanding that he return to a home only vaguely remembered.

He slowly and deliberately took off his clothing, folding each article and placing it neatly on the bank of the water hole. He stood there naked, savoring the anticipation of both the pain of memory and the tactile pleasure of the water. He lay down on his stomach and pushed himself down the bank and into the water. His entry was soft and silent, and only a few ripples disturbed the shadows of the cabbage palms that played across the surface of the water hole.

The moment Albert hit the water, the worries and concerns of past and present disappeared. He was just a creature in the element he was born to inhabit. He didn't need to think; he just needed to do. His webbed feet drove him deeper into the pond with each stroke of his legs. The coolness of the water rippled his fur and washed away the dirt from days of desert travel.

Albert opened his eyes and watched freshwater crayfish dart among the rocks on the bottom of the pond. He grabbed one in his bill, and as he crushed and swallowed it he was overcome by hunger. Without thinking, he used his bill to push over rocks on the bottom of the water hole and ate the earthworms he found. He swam the length of the pool and dived in and out of the reeds on the far bank. Albert chased tadpoles and water beetles through the shallows. He ate what he caught and was excited by those he missed. For the hour he hunted, he wasn't Albert, late of the zoo in Adelaide. He was just an ordinary platypus in a water hole. It was a good feeling.

II

Every Paw Turned Against Him

A faint splashing sound woke Albert from an unsound sleep. He rolled over in the sand and saw TJ kneeling on the bank of the water hole, wringing water out of his long johns. TJ had on his hat, and a blue bandana had been tied around his neck where it partially covered the gunshot wound. His moleskin pants had been washed and were draped across another patch of bottlebrush a few yards from where Albert had been sleeping.

TJ looked over at Albert. "Good morning, sunshine."

He stood up, shook out his underwear, and walked over and put it on the bush next to his pants. TJ looked up at the sun, which had passed midpoint.

"Make that good afternoon. Bring your stuff over to the camp and we'll make a plan." TJ felt his pants to see if they were getting dry, then walked back toward the lean-to.

Albert got up, brushed himself off, and got dressed. By the time he reached the lean-to, TJ was already sitting next to the fire pit pulling things out of the cotton sack.

TJ looked up at Albert. "Sorry to fade on you like that, but I hadn't slept in three days."

Albert sat down across the fire pit from TJ. "What sort of plan are we going to make?"

"I was thinking about revenge and then maybe a holdup or two. I tried claim jumping once, and let me tell you, there ain't no money in it." TJ pulled a can of black powder from the sack.

Albert didn't know who TJ was planning to get even with. On top of that, he didn't know who or what TJ was, or why TJ had gone to the trouble of saving his life. He started to ask TJ but thought better of it. Asking direct questions in Old Australia had usually not provided the answers that Albert hoped for, and he was beginning to believe that the best course was just to let things unfold of their own accord.

"I don't know anything about holdups or claim jumping."

TJ pulled a couple of small lead ingots out of the sack. "Then we'll start with revenge. Nobody chains Terrance James Walcott to a post and gets away with it. I put paid to that damned possum, now it's Bertram's turn. What do you think about burning down the Gates of Hell?"

"I hadn't really thought about it," Albert said honestly.

TJ continued looking through the contents of the sack. "It probably wouldn't be as easy as setting fire to the store at Ponsby Station, not with all the dingoes around, but with a little luck we ought to be able to pull it off."

Albert hadn't been too surprised that TJ knew his name. There was no telling how long TJ had been listening to his conversation with Bertram before the fight in the Gates of Hell. Albert had told Bertram his name, but he was sure he hadn't said anything about Ponsby Station.

"Ponsby Station? I don't think I know the place," Albert said carefully.

"They sure seem to know you." TJ pulled a folded piece of paper out of the sack and passed it over the fire pit to Albert.

Albert unfolded the paper. It was a poster with his name on it.

REWARD
ALBERT THE PLATYPUS WANTED FOR ARSON AND CHEATING AT TWO-UP

With paraffin and malice aforethought,
the above named platypus burned down the
General Mercantile
at Ponsby Station and cheated at two-up

DESCRIPTION
Medium height, webbed feet, has a beak, and
is not a marsupial.
Last seen in the company of a wombat accomplice

FIVE SHILLINGS will be paid for the capture of
said platypus, dead or alive, and delivery of the corpus
to the proper authorities

Sing Sing O'Hanlin, Cap't, Ponsby Station Fusiliers

"It's a bill," said Albert after reading the poster.

"What?"

"I said it's a bill, not a beak." Albert handed the reward poster back to TJ. "That's all I've got to say."

TJ nodded, took the poster, and put it back in the sack. "I like a partner that knows how to keep his mouth shut."

Albert wasn't about to tell TJ that Jack was the one that set the fire. No platypus from Adelaide would betray a friend. Besides, he realized that TJ thought he was a tougher creature than he really was, and there was no reason to let him think differently.

"I'm not used to having a partner," Albert said after a little thought.

TJ looked Albert straight in the eye. "Hell, Albert, we need each other. I don't know straight-up about this place, and from the looks of that poster, you could use someone to watch your back. Furthermore, I've seen you shoot, and you need a lot of help in that direction. Besides, robbery is always more fun if you can talk to someone about it."

After Ponsby Station and the Gates of Hell, Albert knew that getting killed in Old Australia was a lot easier than he had thought. Jack had tried to tell him, but watching Theodore frothing at the mouth had brought it home. Without help, he didn't stand much of a chance of getting to the place he belonged. TJ probably knew more about Old Australia than he did, but Jack had taught him a few things, and that might be enough to hold up his end of any deal with TJ.

"I guess learning to shoot couldn't hurt any," he said.

TJ pulled a tin of percussion caps out of the sack. "I pulled that poster off a gum tree the day before that possum caught me. I was hoping I might run into you. What did you get away with last night, besides your pistol?"

Albert searched through his coat pockets and brought out the Colt, the box of strike-anywhere matches, the gold sovereign, and the piece of oilcloth that Jack had wrapped the pistol in. Albert laid everything on his coat.

"That's the lot, except for an empty canteen."

TJ reached over and picked up the sovereign. He flipped it in the air, caught it, and bit down on the coin. Then he smiled.

"That's the stuff, Albert. It's been awhile since I put a tooth to real gold. Where did you get it?"

"The two-up game in Ponsby Station."

"Did you cheat?"

"I don't think so, but I was drunk at the time."

TJ started laughing. "You're the partner for me, sure enough. Hand me the Colt. I'll clean it up and reload it."

Albert handed TJ the pistol.

"You'd like San Francisco, Albert. Hell of a town. If it hadn't been for letting my guard down, I'd be there yet. Where are you from?"

"Adelaide, and I can do without it," Albert said firmly.

TJ put the gold coin back on Albert's coat, got up, and walked over to where his underwear was drying in the sun. He took it off the bush and brought it back to where he'd been sitting.

"I wasn't always from San Francisco. It's a place you've got to look for."

TJ searched in the sack and pulled out a needle and thread. After a little difficulty he got the needle threaded and began to sew up the hole in the shoulder of his long johns.

"I was born in the forest. I didn't like it much. It always seemed that everywhere I went was twenty miles from nowhere. Learned a few things in the forest, though: how to steal, how to run, and how to fight if I got cornered. All that came in handy when I got to California."

TJ reached over and held up the cotton sack. "I stole all this at the Gates of Hell. I'm glad to see I haven't lost my touch." He put the sack back down and continued: "After I got loose, I snuck back into the building to get my clothes and finish the job I started the night before. Then you showed up and needed a demon. I was glad to oblige."

"Bertram said they didn't sell supplies at the Gates of Hell," Albert remembered.

"Among other things, Bertram's a damn liar." TJ spit into the fire pit and went back to sewing. "They sell what they steal or what they get from the dingoes. Bertram takes it around to other towns and sells it to storekeepers."

"Who told you that?" Albert asked.

"Bertram, of course. That possum was too crazy to hold a conversation." TJ finished sewing up the hole and bit the thread loose from the needle.

"The night before, I had jimmied the lock on the back door of the Gates of Hell and was just getting ready to slip inside when that damned possum snuck up behind me and hit me with a rock. When I woke up, I was chained to a post out in back of the store. Bertram would get bored every so often and come out the store and brag on himself. He talked so much he didn't even notice I had managed get one end of the chain loose."

TJ put the needle and thread back in his sack, stood up, and started putting on his long johns. "They're still a little wet, but they should dry before evening. I can't abide being dirty."

After he finished putting on his underwear, TJ walked over and took his pants off the bush and put them on. "You might want to start collecting some firewood. I'll head over to the far side of the pond and see if I can catch some crawdads for dinner. I didn't have enough time to steal any food."

Spending the rest of his life stealing and shooting was not

what Albert had in mind when he left Adelaide. He still wanted desperately to find the land that he'd dreamed of for so many years, but he wasn't sure anymore what that place might look like. He had assumed that it would be something like where he was born, but he had just spent the morning in a place similar to that, and the experience had left him feeling incomplete. But to doubt in Heaven was not something he could do and still go on.

He was wanted dead or alive in and around Ponsby Station, and that was going to make his journey more difficult, no matter what the destination. With every paw turned against him, shooting and stealing seemed more like educational necessities and a lot less like a couple of bad habits. The time would come for him to move on again; but for now, the valley he was in was world enough. The thought of a fire that night was comforting to him and would be enough to carry him into the uncertainties of another morning.

Fallen tree limbs littered the valley floor, and it took no time to pile up enough firewood for the evening. His days with Jack had given him a sense of how much wood was needed, and he finished the chore with enough time left to explore the valley before it got dark.

He found the spring that fed water into the valley and found more ancient paintings on the cliff walls above the spring. The drawing of a segmented serpent caught his attention at the base of another faint trail a hundred yards ahead.

He made his way up the trail and discovered a rock shelter halfway up the cliff wall, a shallow cave carved into sandstone by eons of wind and rain. Carvings of animals and stick figures of men covered the cliff wall at the entrance.

Albert ducked his head and crawled into the shelter. The ceiling of the shelter had been blackened by fires in the far-distant past. Now, the only inhabitant of the cave was a brown snake coiled in the corner digesting something that had formed a lump halfway down its body.

Albert sat at the mouth of the shelter for a long time, watching the light fade in the valley and wondering whether animals or men had made the drawings that surrounded him.

12

A Paradise Lost

The smell of smoke broke into Albert's thoughts, and he looked down to see TJ feeding branches into a small fire he had started. The snake had stretched itself out along the back wall of the cave and appeared to have gone to sleep.

Albert quietly crawled out of the shelter and made his way down the cliff and across the valley to the fire. TJ had put the crayfish on a large, flat rock that he had slanted toward the fire, and was using the point of his clasp knife to move the ones closest to the flames when it looked like they were starting to burn.

"I used to cook in a mining camp, but the job only lasted two days, so don't expect much." TJ picked up a smaller rock, put some crayfish on it, and passed it to Albert. "Remind me to steal some plates."

Albert ate slowly. He wasn't very hungry after his morning hunt, but crayfish cooked or fresh were a welcome change from sardines.

"Where was the mining camp?" he asked.

TJ scraped the rest of the crayfish into one paw and put down the knife. He juggled the crayfish between paws for a moment to let them cool. "It was a placer claim near Coloma. First job I had after I found California." He began eating the crayfish.

"Did you have a hard time finding California?" Albert put down the rock and held his paws out toward the warmth of the campfire.

"Not really. I just walked away into the forest, got lost for a while, walked through some trees, and there I was."

TJ finished his meal, walked over to the edge of the water hole, and washed the smell of crayfish from his paws. He came back to the fire and continued:

"In the forest you always heard things about a place where things were a lot different, a place where animals got to shoot back. First time I heard the story, I said to myself, That's the place for Terrance James Walcott. Stealing bird's eggs and running from dogs might be good enough for other raccoons, but I wanted the big time, and by God, California was the place."

TJ reached in his sack and pulled out a pint bottle of whiskey. "Drink?"

Albert shook his head.

"You should have seen San Francisco, Albert. Gold coming in from the mines around the city, ships in the harbor, gambling and drinking started at noon. Every badger, weasel, and bunco artist from miles down the coast hung out there. Every night was Saturday, and shootings were a dime a dozen. It was a paradise, let me tell you."

TJ looked wistful and took a long pull on the bottle.

Albert wasn't sure what badgers, weasels, and bunco artists were, but he assumed they were animals that lived in California. San Francisco didn't seem very paradise-like to him, but good or bad it was at least a world that was different from the one he had found when he left the zoo. If there were two places that were different from Adelaide, there were bound to be others—and if so, it was just a matter of walking far enough in the right direction until he found the one he wanted.

"When I find paradise, I'm not leaving," Albert said, thinking out loud.

TJ put the cork back in the bottle. "You might, if one dark night a mob with flour sacks on their heads started chasing you down a wharf."

He put the bottle back in his sack and took out a small pot and one of the lead ingots. "Every once in a while virtue gets out of hand, even in San Francisco. One day you're a customer, the next day you're on a list of bad apples." TJ put the ingot into the pot and placed the pot on the coals at the edge of the fire. "The local feather merchants stop watering their whiskey long enough to form a Vigilance Committee. They lynch a few creatures, just to show their wives that they believe in law and order, and then go back to making money off sin and greed."

TJ took a small ladle out of the sack and put it in the pot with the lead. "I got caught up in the annual frenzy of piety, and if it hadn't been for a strange ship at the end of that wharf, I would have ended up decorating a lamppost."

He was quiet for a while as he sat watching the lead melt into a bright silver puddle. When the lead was completely melted, TJ took a bullet mould out of the sack and began ladling the molten lead into it. Albert had watched Jack make bullets for his pepperbox pistol one evening, but TJ seemed more at home with the process.

"I ran up the gangplank of that ship with the mob a hundred yards behind me. The second I got on board I pulled a pistol, hoping they would have to come at me one at a time. I turned to shoot the first one up the gangplank, when a bank of fog closed over the ship and the wharf disappeared. That scared the hell out of me, let me tell you."

When the mould was full, TJ set it by the fire, then took off the bandana from around his neck and spread it out in front of him. "I could hear paws running along the deck and hear the captain yell up to sailors in the rigging, but I couldn't see a damned soul. Pretty soon I heard water running under the keel and knew we were under sail. Every so often I could see a faint image of some animal, but the image would fade as soon as I took a second look. I wandered around. I looked in the hold. I looked in the captain's cabin. The whole ship was empty, and except for the voices and the shadows there was no sign of life, no water, no supplies, no nothing. The fog covered everything. I couldn't see the sails, and I couldn't see beyond the railings. I sat down with my back against the quarterdeck and put my pistol in my lap. I didn't think the gun would have done much good, but it's hard to shake the habit of a lifetime.

"After a few hours, the ship became very quiet, and I couldn't hear the voices anymore. I stayed awake as long as I could, but running from a mob and hunting ghosts had taken the starch out of me. I went to sleep, and when I woke up, here I was."

TJ picked up the bullet mould and used the ladle handle to knock off the sprue. He opened the mould and let a pistol ball fall out on the bandana. He closed the mould and used the ladle to fill the mould again.

"Actually, I was off the coast of somewhere I'd never seen before. But I didn't care. I knew I didn't belong on the damned ship. I jumped overboard and swam in—lost my pistol in the surf, but at least I didn't drown."

TJ continued to cast pistol balls and drop them on the

bandana. "I walked inland looking for fresh water. It was harder to find than I thought, and if it hadn't been for Muldoon, I would have died for sure." TJ picked up one of the bullets and examined it in the firelight. He grunted in satisfaction. "I was always better at making bullets than I was at cooking."

"Muldoon?" Albert blurted out.

TJ dropped the bullet back on the bandana. "Strange creature, Muldoon. I felt a little sorry for him."

"I heard about Muldoon from a friend of mine. He wanted me to give him a message," Albert said excitedly.

"Muldoon is long gone, Albert. He doesn't like company much." TJ used the edge of the sack to protect his paw from the heat and lifted the lead pot off the coals. "I walked into the desert through a cut in the mountains along the coast. I was three days without water when I saw his tent."

"A tent?"

"Muldoon lives in an old circus tent with yellow-and-red stripes. It kind of stands out."

"What's he like? My friend Jack didn't talk about him very much."

"Well, he was an animal I'd never seen before, but that's true about everyone I've met since I got here. He looked like he had seen better days, that's for sure. He kept to himself and didn't seem much interested in conversation."

TJ put the bullet mould and the cast bullets in the cotton sack. "I doubt he was handsome when he was young, and now he's blind in one eye and covered with scars. Ugly as he is, he was there when I needed him, and I owe him. He gave me water and led me to this valley. He told me about the dingoes and the Gates of Hell."

"Where did he go?" Albert asked.

"I don't know. He just brought me to the trail that leads up here and then walked away. I never really got a chance to thank him. He only asked me one thing the two days we were together." TJ stood up. "I'm going to call it a night."

Albert looked up from the fire. "What did he ask?"

"He asked me if I had any sardines."

13

Bushrangers

S tand and deliver," said TJ, and cocked his pistol for emphasis.
The wallaby looked confused.

"Put your paws in the air," Albert added.

"Oh, it's robbery," the wallaby said, and raised his arms.

"It's not an ice-cream social, bunny." TJ pushed his pistol into the wallaby's nose.

"Actually, the name's Ralph," said the wallaby.

"Don't get smart with me, Ralph. Where I come from, anyone with a snout like yours is a rabbit." TJ squinted at Ralph's nose.

"What's a rabbit?" asked the wallaby.

"Damn it! If I'd wanted to be paid by the hour, I would have gone to work for the railroad. Now, let's get down to it. You got five seconds. Fork over the cash or your next hop will be on the far side of the pearly gates."

Albert could tell that TJ was becoming impatient. The wallaby was their third victim in as many days, and so far they had managed to steal a worn blanket and a bag of rock candy.

Ralph put his paws down and pulled a small coin purse from the pocket of his waistcoat. As he snapped open the purse, he cocked his head and looked at Albert.

"You're Albert the Platypus, aren't you?"

Albert wasn't quite sure what to say. "It depends on who's asking."

"I knew it. I can't wait to tell the wife."

TJ shook his head disgustedly and took his pistol out of Ralph's nose. He uncocked it and put it back in the pocket of his pants. "I'm glad my mother didn't live to see this," he muttered. Then he walked over to a large rock by the trail and sat down.

"I've never been robbed by anybody famous before," Ralph continued as he pulled a small coin out of the coin purse and extended it to Albert. "I recognized you immediately."

Albert took the coin. Not knowing what else to do, he reached into his pocket and took out the paper sack of rock candy he and TJ had taken from a sugar glider the day before. He held out the sack. "Have some candy, Ralph."

The wallaby closed his coin purse and put it back in his waistcoat. He reached into the paper sack. "The minute I saw the reward poster, I said to myself, Any creature, marsupial or not, that burned down Ponsby Station can't be all bad. The place had a less than stellar reputation." Ralph took a piece of candy and put it in his pocket next to his coin purse. "If you're finished with the robbery, I really must be off. The wife hates it when I'm late for supper."

The wallaby tipped his bowler to Albert and started down the trail, being careful to give TJ a wide berth.

After much discussion, TJ had decided to stage a few robberies before trying to even his score with Bertram. It would give Albert time to learn the trade and provide them with needed supplies and maybe a little cash. Muldoon had told TJ that there was a series of small towns and mining camps that circled the desert between the distant mountain and the Gates of Hell.

Trails and small roads linked the towns around the desert, and TJ thought ambushing travelers on one of the roads might prove profitable.

Albert wasn't keen on being a thief, but during his time in the desert, almost everyone he had met had made their living by stealing, cheating, gambling, or burning things down. Now that he had been labeled a cheat and an arsonist, it was only a small step to theft and a life of crime, an occupation that seemed to be much favored in the region. Jack and TJ made their living by dishonest means, but they were his friends, and thieves and killers like Bertram and Theodore weren't. Albert had come to the conclusion that another key to survival in Old Australia was in picking a criminal element you liked and sticking with it.

Also, Albert wasn't sure if he had the makings of a good thief. So far his life of crime had consisted of standing around while TJ did most of the work. He hadn't gotten a chance to draw his pistol, and wearing a mask seemed a little silly given the bill that stuck out in front of his face.

After Ralph disappeared down the road, Albert walked over to TJ, who had calmed down and now looked more disgusted than angry.

"How much did we get?"

Albert looked at the coin in his paw. "A tuppence."

TJ took off his hat and wiped his brow with the sleeve of his long johns. "If there is a sorrier place than this for honest robbery, I don't know of one. We're going to have to think of something else." He looked up at the sun. "We've got a few hours before dark. Let's try and get a little sleep before we head back."

Albert and TJ had crossed the desert from the water hole two nights before and had been making a cold camp in the hills above the road. It was too dangerous to cross the desert during the day, and even a night crossing had brought them too close for comfort to one of the packs of dingoes that roamed that part of the Outback. The only advantage they had was TJ's night vision, and it had seen them safely across the desert one more time.

TJ stood up and walked out of sight of the road and around some large rocks to where they had left what few possessions they had. Albert followed him off the road.

"You can have the blanket." TJ sat down with his back to one of the rocks that had been warmed by the sun and tipped his hat over his eyes.

Albert took a drink from his canteen and then carried the stolen blanket to a sandy spot that was shaded from the afternoon sun. He lay down in the sand. The quiet of the afternoon was disturbed by the buzz of an occasional fly, but the insects were a normal part of life on the desert and Albert had learned to ignore them. He knew that he and TJ would have a long and dangerous trek back to the water hole that night and that getting a few hours' rest was a good idea. Still, it was hard for him to fall asleep.

Albert had gotten as far as he had with only bits and pieces of information. It had started with the rumors and fantasies about Old Australia he had heard at the zoo, and continued with Jack's stories about how animals got to this part of Old Australia. Jack had told him that Muldoon thought everyone that walked far enough ended up here, but TJ had gotten here by boat and Albert had gotten here with the help of the South Australia railway. There didn't seem to be any rhyme nor reason as to why some animals got to Old Australia and some didn't. Muldoon might have some answers, but it was unlikely that Albert would find him anytime soon.

TJ hadn't been able to tell Albert much about Muldoon,

except that he had been badly hurt sometime in the past and didn't like the company of other animals. Muldoon had referred to the desert between the Gates of Hell and the distant mountain as Hell itself and had told TJ that most animals from that part of Old Australia never came there. Those that did didn't survive very long.

Albert wanted to know how Muldoon had survived in Hell for so long, but TJ didn't have an answer. Albert also wanted to know what had happened between Jack and Muldoon and why Jack wouldn't talk about it. He fell asleep still wondering.

He began to dream, and those dreams became a kaleidoscope of his time in Old Australia: bottles of beer flying from train windows, Theodore screaming "Zoo!" Jack singing off-key, sand blowing so hard he couldn't see; the taste of gin, the flash of pistol shots, coins flying in the lamplight of Ponsby Station, and the yelling of the crowd.

The yelling woke Albert up. Albert opened his eyes and saw that TJ had disappeared. The sounds of a struggle were coming from the road beyond the rocks. Albert jumped to his feet, pulled his pistol, and ran around the rocks onto the road.

TJ was standing in the middle of the road holding a bandicoot by the throat with his left paw and trying to pistol-whip it with the gun in his right paw. Another bandicoot had TJ around the neck and was hanging off his back, biting TJ's ear hard enough to draw blood. TJ's hat lay on the side of the road next to an old Enfield carbine and a couple of jute bags.

Albert fired his pistol into the middle of the road, and the yelling stopped. The fighters froze and looked over at where Albert was standing and then they all started yelling again.

"Hit this one in the head!" TJ yelled as he flung the bandicoot with his left paw in Albert's direction.

The bandicoot on TJ's back spit the ear out of his mouth and yelled, "Albert! It's us!"

At the mention of Albert's name the fighting stopped again. Albert looked down at the bandicoot that had just landed in front of him.

"Roger?"

"Too right," said the bandicoot as he stood up and started brushing himself off.

Alvin dropped off TJ's back and ran over to where Albert and Roger were standing.

"It's good to see you, mate," said Alvin as he grabbed Albert's paw and started shaking it.

"We've come to sign up," Roger joined in. "We want to be bushrangers."

Before Albert could say anything, both bandicoots began talking at once.

"We heard you were around here. A sugar glider showed up at Ponsby Station and said he'd been robbed by a platypus on the road to Barton Springs," Alvin said excitedly.

"I said, 'That's our old mate, Albert,'" Roger interrupted.

Alvin nodded. "That's what he said for a fact."

"And Alvin said, 'Let's go have a drink with Albert,'" Roger continued.

"We grabbed our swag and came straightaway," Alvin joined in.

"The wallaby up the road said you were close by. When we got here, we were set on by that bloody foreigner." Roger pointed over to where TJ was picking up his hat.

TJ put on his hat and, from the look on his face, was considering shooting both bandicoots in the back. "Those rodents better be good friends of yours, Albert. If not, I'm going to have their guts for garters."

Both Alvin and Roger bristled.

"Fat bloody chance," said Alvin.

"Before you showed up, Albert, we had him cold," added Roger.

"Fair dinkum, and we can do it again." Alvin spit in both his paws and started toward TJ.

Albert grabbed Alvin by the back of his collar. "Who else was at Ponsby Station when the sugar glider showed up?"

"O'Hanlin and his bullyboys. They're trying to rebuild the mercantile with the help of some of the miners."

Albert looked over at TJ. "Do you think that might be a problem?"

14

Last Stand of the Fusiliers

Albert heard another shot from the Enfield, followed by the rattle of musketry. The shooting was getting closer, and darkness was still a half an hour away. Albert led Alvin and Roger out of the hills and onto the flats of Hell.

There hadn't been much time. O'Hanlin and the Ponsby Station Fusiliers had been only minutes behind the bandicoots. Albert and TJ had just retrieved their gear when the first kangaroo appeared on the road. TJ had grabbed the carbine from Roger and fired a shot in the general direction of the scout.

TJ's shot delayed the pursuit long enough for them to herd the bandicoots off the road and into the hills. TJ thought that the Fusiliers wouldn't follow them any farther than the edge of Hell because of the dingoes. They just needed time to get there. They agreed that Albert and the bandicoots would head directly through the desert toward the water hole, while TJ would try to slow down the pursuers. TJ took a handful of paper cartridges from Roger's bag and disappeared into the brush above the trail.

That had been an hour ago, and Albert and the bandicoots had been on the run the whole time. Roger and Alvin were not in the best of shape, and Albert was now carrying both bags of their gear. The bandicoots were panting continuously and occasionally missed their footing.

"Be a mate, Albert. Let's give it a rest." Roger was sweating, and his sweat smelled of cheap gin.

"It's not much farther—you can make it." Albert slowed his pace, but the bandicoots still had difficulty keeping up. Alvin and Roger couldn't keep going much longer, but he also knew that the deeper they went into the desert, the better chance they would have to see the next morning.

Albert felt sorry for Roger and Alvin, but sympathy wasn't of much use in desperate circumstances. TJ was doing his job, and it was up to Albert to do his. Albert needed to get the bandicoots to cover somewhere in the flats of Hell and somewhere beyond rifle shot of the hills behind him. Albert wasn't sure how far a rifle could shoot, so the farther the better.

For the first time in his life, Albert was responsible for the lives of others, and the effect of that responsibility surprised him. He had ceased thinking of the bandicoots as friends. They had become objects that he was duty-bound to deliver safely. Friendship and sympathy had no place in the equation. All he could do was to keep pushing them to their destination regardless of the pain and discomfort it might cause them. Alvin and Roger had stood by him when friends had been in short supply, and he would stand by them now. If they didn't make it to safety, it wouldn't be because Albert hadn't given everything he had.

He eventually paused to allow each of the bandicoots a small drink of water. The shooting had stopped, and all he could hear was the sound of the wind blowing across the flats of Hell.

Low hills lay behind and to the left of them. The top of the distant mountain rose from beyond the far horizon. Termite mounds and scattered scrub covered the desert floor all the way to a stand of stunted red river gum trees growing along a dry creekbed at the base of the hills to their left. Except for the distant mountain, Albert didn't recognize any other landmarks. He knew that if he kept the hills on his left and the mountain ahead of him, he would eventually come to the trail that led up the cliff walls.

Albert had just started moving toward the creek when he heard a whistle, and he turned to see TJ running toward them across the flats. His hat was hanging from his neck by the chinstrap, and he had a bandana tied around his head. TJ was carrying the Enfield in his right paw, and his face was streaked with powder residue from the rifle.

"They're not stopping," TJ said as he slowed to a walk next to Albert.

"I was heading over there." Albert pointed to the gum trees.

TJ shook his head. "You haven't got enough time. Go another hundred yards and fort up behind a termite mound. When it gets dark, move down the creek and into the trees. Be quiet and wait for me there." Without another word TJ started running toward the trees.

Alvin started jogging toward a clump of termite mounds that lay at an oblique angle from the grove of trees. As he trotted on, he could hear the rattled breath of the bandicoots behind him. Albert had just reached the mounds when he heard Alvin squeak. He looked back to see Roger lying on the ground. Albert dropped the sacks behind one of the mounds and ran back to where Alvin was trying to drag Roger to his feet.

Roger's breathing was ragged and shallow. It was obvious that Roger had reached the end of his run. Albert grabbed the back of Roger's overalls and dragged him across the ground to where he had left the sacks. Alvin hovered behind them.

With a final rush of adrenaline, Albert got Roger behind the termite mound and let go of his overalls.

Alvin sat down next to Roger. "Is he all right?"

"He's fine, just tired," Albert whispered. He poured some water on Roger's head and neck, and Roger began to breathe a little easier.

"Lie down. Don't talk and don't move. If Roger starts to moan, put your paw over his mouth."

Albert handed the canteen to Alvin and lay down behind the termite mound. It wasn't five minutes before the wind carried the sound of voices to where they were. The voices got louder, and Albert pulled himself up on the base of the mound and looked back across the desert.

The Ponsby Station Fusiliers were milling around where TJ had parted company with Albert. They were searching the ground and babbling to one another. Albert was sure they were looking for tracks, and if the light hadn't been failing they would have already found what they were looking for.

Up close the Fusiliers were not particularly impressive. O'Hanlin had on a hussar's jacket two sizes too big for him and a shako on his head that kept slipping onto his glasses. He was using an artillery sword to direct the search. The body of the troop consisted of a dozen kangaroos and rock wallabies, all wearing bits and pieces of old uniforms. They were armed with a varied collection of muskets and pistols with which they seemed to have only a passing familiarity.

One of the rock wallabies found what he thought was a track, which immediately started an argument as to what kind of track it was and who might have made it. The Fusiliers all gathered around the track to offer an opinion. Before a definitive answer was arrived at, the meeting was interrupted by the boom of the

Enfield. A rifle ball hummed over the heads of the Fusiliers, and Albert could see powder smoke drifting out of the stand of gum trees.

After a moment of confusion, the Fusiliers fired a ragged volley at the trees and charged toward TJ's position, with O'Hanlin in the lead waving his sword. Albert watched for the ten minutes it took them to reach the tree line and then slid back down the termite mound to where Roger and Alvin were lying.

Roger had opened his eyes, and Alvin was giving him some water from the canteen. Albert looked over at Roger. "How do you feel?"

Roger raised his head. "I need a drink really bad, Albert."

"Not now, Roger."

Albert crawled back up on the base of the termite mound. He watched the stand of trees, but he couldn't see any movement. After a few minutes he looked behind him. Except for some patches of brush, it was a clear run to the creekbed, and Albert felt he wouldn't have any trouble getting there, even in the dark.

Albert waited on the mound until the twilight turned to darkness. Roger and Alvin were sitting quietly behind him, and it looked like they could travel when the time came. Albert was starting to crawl down from the mound when he noticed lights coming from the gum trees. The lights flickered from behind the trees, and the smell of campfires drifted across the termite mound.

Someone had set up camp in the grove of trees, and it was a safe bet that that someone wasn't TJ. He and Albert hadn't started a fire since they'd left the water hole. Assuming that TJ was still alive, any rendezvous with him in the grove that night was now impossible. Albert had a choice: he could head back out into the flats, circle around the trees, and pick up the trail along the base of the hills; or he could take Roger and Alvin to the dry creek. Once in the creekbed, he could leave the bandicoots long enough to search for TJ.

Albert looked out across the flats and thought he saw movement near one of the termite mounds. It was dark, but there was enough starlight to outline the mounds against the sky. Albert kept watching and soon saw another shadow move among the mounds in the direction of the grove of trees. The wind was still coming from the direction of the campfires, and it wouldn't carry any smell of Albert or the bandicoots to where he could see movement. Albert lay absolutely still and waited.

The moving outlines finally got between Albert and the gum trees, and the wind carried a new smell in Albert's direction. It was the smell of dog, mixed with the smell of the wood smoke from the campfires. It was the second time that Albert had smelled dingoes from close up, and this time he had better control of his emotions. The spurs on his hind legs still extended themselves, but the feelings of fear and anger were replaced by a steady calculation.

Now he had no choice. He would have to take the bandicoots to the creekbed, then try to find TJ. Albert took another long look into the night, then slid back down the mound to Alvin and Roger.

"Not a word, not a sound," Albert whispered.

Alvin and Roger nodded. They were either too tired to complain or they had gotten a smell of the dingoes. In either case, they were as subdued as Albert had ever seen them.

Albert carefully picked up the jute bags and began walking toward the creek as quietly as he could. Roger and Alvin fell in behind him.

Albert couldn't see well in the dark and had to depend on his memory and sense of smell to get them there. The smell of wood smoke had become stronger and had blotted out any other smells on the night wind. Albert worried that he might walk right up on a dingo without knowing it, so he took his time. He stopped every few yards to peer into the darkness ahead of him. The hills beyond the creekbed were silhouetted by the sky and kept him going in the right direction.

Albert reached the creek and stopped by a patch of brush. He handed Alvin and Roger the jute bags.

"Lie down under the brush," he whispered. "I'll be back as soon as I can."

"What if you don't come back?" Alvin whispered back.

"Do the best you can to get back to the road." Albert handed his pistol to Alvin and started down the creekbed toward the campfires. He knew the pistol wouldn't do Alvin any good, but he hoped it would make him feel better.

Albert moved slowly. The smell of smoke became stronger, and he could hear voices coming from the camp. It was the Fusiliers laughing and talking. Every so often the sound of O'Hanlin's voice could be heard above the rest. Albert was too far away to make out what they were saying, but he was as close to the Fusiliers as he wanted to get. He turned to start back up the way he'd come when TJ whispered to him:

"What took you so long?"

TJ had walked up behind Albert, close enough to touch him. "Dingoes."

There was a moment of silence, then TJ murmured, "Where?"

"They were moving across the desert toward the trees." Albert pointed out into the blackness of the flats of Hell.

"I didn't think they'd get here that fast. Where are the rodents?" TJ took the bandana off his head and put it in his pocket.

"I left them a little way up the creek."

"Go get them and take them up to the base of the hills as quickly as you can. Wait there and I'll find you. Whatever you do, don't come back this way." TJ put his hat on and walked through the brush onto the flats.

Albert got back to where Alvin and Roger were hiding under the brush. He took his pistol back from Alvin and made sure it wasn't cocked. He had made a mistake by firing his pistol to break up the fight between TJ and the bandicoots. It had pinpointed their location to the Fusiliers, and he didn't want to make the same mistake a second time.

He got the bandicoots out of the creek and led them up to the base of the hills, high enough to be able to see the fires of the camp. They were too far away to make out individuals, but they could see movement around the fires. Occasionally, a snatch of laughter or conversation would reach them, carried on the wind.

Albert looked back down into the creekbed and saw that it had become full of shadows moving toward the fires. Two of the shadows stopped at the clump of brush where he had hidden the bandicoots. The shadows put their noses in the air. After a moment one of the shadows moved on, but the second one began to circle the brush and then started zigzagging across the creekbed toward the hills. It stopped for a moment at the edge of the creek and put its nose in the air again. It hesitated and then turned to head back down up the creek to the camp. That was when Roger coughed.

The shadow spun around and bounded up the hill. Albert jumped to his feet, keeping himself between the shadow and the bandicoots. The dingo was on him in a matter of seconds. Instinctively, Albert threw his hat into the dingo's face. The dingo reared up on his hind legs and swung at Albert with a stone club. Albert ducked, and before the dingo could swing again, a rock sailed out of the darkness and hit him in the back. The dingo growled and turned toward the new assailant. Albert threw himself on the dingo's back and drove his spurs into his flanks.

Albert had been there once before, those many years ago on the banks of the Murray. He remembered his mother's torn body lying along the bank and the smell of frightened dog. The rage consumed him once again. He drove his spurs into the flanks of the dingo, one after the other like he was climbing a tree. The dingo dropped his club and tried to dislodge the enraged platypus. The dingo was still trying to reach Albert when TJ emerged from the darkness and cut his throat.

TJ took the bandana out of his pocket and wiped the blade of his pocketknife. He folded the knife, then bent over and picked up Albert's hat. He walked back into the darkness and reappeared a few moments later carrying the carbine. TJ stood on the hillside looking toward the fires of the Fusiliers.

Albert lay on the dingo's body, shaking with rage. Blood was seeping onto the ground all around him. Albert hated the smell of both the blood and the dingo, but he couldn't force himself to move. For the first time, he could remember everything about his mother's death and how he had thrown himself on the dog that killed her. They weren't good memories, but they were real, and no longer the unconnected flashes of horror that had haunted him for all those years in the zoo. The sound of gunshots in the distance brought him back to Old Australia.

Albert staggered to his feet. TJ didn't say anything. He just handed Albert his hat and pointed over to the grove of trees where the Fusiliers were camped. Shadows danced in and out of the campsite; there were flashes of pistol shots, and the yelling of the maimed and the dying. The fight didn't last very long, and soon the sounds of guns and struggle were replaced by screams of pain.

The screaming went on for what seemed like hours, and the wind carried the smell of burned hair, blood, and fear to where TJ and Albert were standing. After the screaming stopped it was another hour before they saw the shadows begin to slip away down the creekbed and across the desert.

TJ waited for a while after the last shadow passed, then motioned for Albert and the bandicoots to follow him back down to the creekbed. Alvin and Roger carried their jute bags close to their bodies as they started down the hill. The bandicoots kept glancing nervously at the body of the dingo as they walked by it, as if they were afraid that it might come to life again. As soon as they passed the body, they hurried ahead and tried to stay as close to TJ and Albert as they could.

They walked slowly toward the camp. The base of the hills came down to the edge of the creekbed and limited their passage to the sandy creek bottom. They could still see the glow and smell the smoke of the smoldering campfires.

The body of a dingo lay next to the trunk of a gum tree at the edge of the camp. Someone had scattered red ochre around the body.

"At least they got one," TJ observed quietly as he walked past the body into the middle of the campsite.

Bits and pieces of the Fusiliers were scattered about the camp. The dingoes had carried off their guns and equipment, and left only the heads and paws of the Fusiliers they had butchered. The smell of charred flesh still hung above the camp.

O'Hanlin's head had been placed on a log. The dingoes had taken his shako, but his spectacles remained on his nose, and the glowing embers of the fires were reflected in the lenses.

15

On Brown Snakes and Bandicoots

Albert stood at the top of the trail that led up from the flats to the entrance of the opening in the cliff. He had taken to coming here each evening to look at the sun setting on the desert below. He would stand there while the shadows lengthened across the flats, then watch them slowly disappear as the sun reached the horizon.

The play of light fascinated Albert. Every day the sun shifted position in the sky ever so slightly, and the movement of the light on the desert changed with it. The change from one day to the next was too subtle to see, but Albert could feel it. He would stand there until the top of the distant mountain faded into an outline in the dusk surrounded by the first few stars of the coming night.

Albert had made the mistake of staying too long one evening. The stars had kept him on top of the trail until nightfall. When he looked down from the sky he saw the campfires of the dingoes on the desert floor.

He didn't like being reminded of what he had seen that night in the stand of gum trees. There was always the chance that the same thing could happen to him or to his friends. Albert knew that the end of the Fusiliers had resulted from their own folly, but that wasn't to say that bad luck wouldn't have worked just as well, and bad luck could happen to anyone.

It had taken them another day and night to get back to the water hole from the Fusilier encampment. There had been only a few hours of darkness left the night of the massacre, and they had gone to ground before dawn the following morning. They waited on a brush-covered rise in the heat of a long day. Albert or TJ would keep watch while the other rested in what little shade was provided by the brush. The bandicoots were quiet and spent most of their time under a stunted desert oak on the back side of the rise.

Roger had started taking nips from a pint bottle he had in his bag the minute the sun came up, and if TJ hadn't taken the bottle away from him, he would have been drunk by noon. Roger gave up the gin without a murmur. After watching what had happened to the dingo that had attacked them the night before, neither Alvin nor Roger were inclined to argue with TJ.

Albert really didn't know what to do with the bandicoots. There hadn't been time to sort things out on the road to Barton Springs. One minute Alvin and Roger had been fighting with TJ and the next minute they had been running for their lives. If he'd had time to think about it, he probably wouldn't have taken them along. The bandicoots were just looking for someone to drink with. The idea of being bushrangers had probably been appealing in a barroom somewhere, but Albert could have told them that the reality of life on the flats of Hell was not what they had in mind. In any case, it had been too late to send them back.

Albert and TJ managed to get the bandicoots to the water hole the next night. After they arrived, TJ immediately set off to wash and clean his gear while Albert started a fire. Alvin made a halfhearted attempt to help gather firewood, but Roger just sat by the fire circle and tried to keep his paws from shaking.

Nothing much was said that night. Everyone was hungry, but it was too dark and they were too tired to try to catch anything for dinner. Alvin and Roger had only brought a little flour and baking powder with them, and nothing to cook it in. Albert passed around the last of the rock candy. After it was eaten, everyone—everyone but Roger—sat quietly around the fire.

After a while, TJ got tired of watching Roger shake and gave him back the bottle of gin. Roger took a few stiff drinks, then lay on his side by the fire and went to sleep. Albert and TJ drifted away soon afterward and left Alvin sitting next to his snoring companion.

The first few days after their return were spent trying to refit as best they could. TJ washed all his clothes and, while they were drying, helped Albert catch crayfish in the water hole. Enough firewood was gathered for a week, and a few failed attempts at biscuits were made. Roger and Alvin recovered quickly and were soon bragging about what they would do to the next dingo that came their way.

Albert spent his mornings swimming in the water hole, and in the early afternoons would walk up the trail near the spring and sit in the rock shelter above the camp. He thought there might be a chance that if he sat there long enough, the stones around him would begin to speak. So far the stones had remained mute, but Albert was happy enough to sit in the silence.

Within a few minutes of his arrival, the brown snake would crawl into the shelter from a crevice in the shelter floor. The snake seemed to be attracted by the heat of Albert's body or perhaps by the noise he made on his hike up the trail. Albert was always glad for quiet company and had begun to think of the snake as some kind of totem sent by their common ancestors. The snake would coil up in the corner of the cave and remain there until Albert left.

After leaving the shelter, Albert would nap in the shade of a saltbush until the sun began to set, and then walk up to the opening in the cliff that looked out across the desert.

Just before dark, Albert would come back to the camp and eat the crayfish that TJ had cooked on the rocks by the fire. Roger and Alvin were always on time for every meal, and after eating as many crayfish as TJ would allow them, they would pass around the bottle.

It had now been four days since their return to the water hole, and both crayfish and gin were running low. Regardless of the danger involved, they decided to leave the next evening, cross the flats, and walk the road to Barton Springs. They needed food and supplies, and Barton Springs was the closest place to get both. TJ had briefly considered a raid on the Gates of Hell, but having the bandicoots along made it a dubious proposition and TJ abandoned the idea.

Robbing travelers on the road had not proven a very successful way of getting resupplied. They needed a better source, and according to the bandicoots there was a large general store in Barton Springs. Any robbery of the store would most likely result in another pursuit, and TJ and Albert wanted to avoid that if they could. Albert suggested that they send the bandicoots into Barton Springs with his gold sovereign to purchase what they needed. Once they had new packs, blankets, and food, they would be in a better position to run or fight, should it come to that.

Aside from Jack's company, the thing that Albert had missed most since he left Ponsby Station was hot tea from the billycan every morning. He hoped there would be enough money left, after they got necessities, for the purchase of a proper teakettle, some loose tea, and cups.

Albert didn't look forward to another night march across the flats of Hell, but in many ways he was glad to be leaving the little valley. He was bothered that he had created a routine that repeated itself on a daily basis, first the water hole, then to the cave, and from there to the opening in the cliff. He had spent too many days walking the limits of his cage in Adelaide not to recognize a similar pattern. It was getting time for him to move on again, but he needed supplies, and he needed to see the bandicoots safely out of Hell.

Albert watched the sun reach the far horizon and the shadows and the light end their dance across the flats. The distant mountain slowly vanished, and Albert turned to hurry back to camp before any fires could be lit in the darkness below the cliff.

16

The Platypus Gang

The bandicoots were three hours late and someone was going to have to find out why. TJ thought that if he pulled his hat down low over the black mask of fur across his eyes he might not stand out that much. Other animals in Old Australia were ring-tailed and had pointed noses and ears.

There was no question about Albert going into Barton Springs. His bill and webbed feet would make him an object of curiosity the minute he hit town. There was also the matter of the reward poster, which was probably still floating around with his description on it. If anyone was to go into Barton Springs, it would have to be TJ.

The trip to Barton Springs from the water hole had been surprisingly easy. TJ had crossed the flats enough times to be able to lead the party through the night with little hesitation. The pace was slower than it had been when they were being chased by the Ponsby Station Fusiliers, and the bandicoots had been able to keep up without too much difficulty. There had been no sign of dingoes near the trail along the foothills, and TJ had cut back into the flats before they reached the massacre site.

They had reached the Barton Springs road before dawn,

rested in a gully off the road for a few hours, then sent Alvin and Roger into town to get the supplies. Albert had made sure that the bandicoots knew exactly what they needed to buy from the store and could repeat the list of the supplies back to him without error. TJ remained quiet, but he was obviously troubled about sending them into town by themselves, and he'd kept Roger's carbine to ensure his return.

But there really hadn't been any choice. It would take both bandicoots to carry the packs and supplies they needed, and to send them into town one at a time would just double the risk. After the bandicoots left, TJ said there was no point in taking chances, and he took Albert to a different location in the hills, on the other side of the road, where they could watch the road near the gully from a distance.

The road to Barton Springs was well traveled, and Albert and TJ watched several parties of marsupials move up and down the road that afternoon. With a professional eye, TJ marked out where it would be best to conduct a holdup and where best to place a lookout to prevent being surprised by other travelers.

Albert spent the afternoon thinking about what he should do next. Once he had a pack and a teakettle, there would be nothing stopping him from continuing his search for a different Old Australia. Maybe TJ would want to come with him, and together they might find a way for TJ to get back to California. With enough food and a friend, there were few things that couldn't be accomplished.

As the afternoon progressed, TJ became more and more restless. Just before dusk, TJ couldn't stand the inaction any longer and decided it was time to search the town for Alvin and Roger. If he couldn't find the bandicoots, TJ planned to break into the general store. He and Albert needed food and supplies. If Alvin and Roger weren't going to deliver them, stealing them was their only option.

TJ left Albert with the worn blanket and one canteen. If he didn't return by the next morning, Albert was to make his way back across the flats of Hell and wait for TJ at the water hole. If Albert was careful, waited until nightfall, and kept to the trail along the hills, he should make the camp by the end of another night. Whoever got to the camp first would wait three days. After that, the survivor would be on his own.

TJ checked the percussion caps on his pistol and the one on the carbine, then pulled his hat down low over his eyes. He took Albert's paw in his own and shook it. "Take care of yourself, partner."

"The same to you, TJ. See you soon," Albert said quietly.

"I'll be back with those damn rodents before midnight."

TJ put the carbine under one arm and started toward Barton Springs. From a distance he was difficult to distinguish from many marsupials, and Albert felt better about his chances of getting into the town undetected.

Midnight came and went and neither the bandicoots nor TJ appeared on the road near the gully. Albert moved closer to the road so he wouldn't miss TJ's or the bandicoots' return. He kept looking into the darkness and hoping that each imagined noise was the first sign of his friends' return. It was a long night.

At dawn, he moved back into the hills where he had been with TJ the day before, and continued to wait. Albert knew that something had gone wrong in Barton Springs. But for now, there was nothing he could do about it.

He decided that it was best to wait until late afternoon and then head back to the water hole, as he and TJ had agreed on. TJ had proven resourceful enough in the past, and there was a good chance he would get back to the valley in the cliffs before Albert could. If TJ failed to appear in three days, Albert would return to Barton Springs and look for him, regardless of the danger involved.

The road was clear when Albert came out of the hills and walked toward the gully. From the gully to the flats of Hell was about a three-hour trek. It would be dark by then and would allow Albert to start immediately across the flats to the water hole.

Albert was halfway down the gully when he heard a voice.

"A platypus returning to the scene of the crime. How trite."

Albert looked over and saw Bertram looking down at him from the lip of the gully. Standing next to Bertram was Theodore. They were both wearing black vests and slouch hats. Theodore was wearing goggles with smoked lenses and pointing a double-barreled shotgun at Albert. Peeking from behind Bertram and Theodore was a group of wallabies, kangaroos, and bandicoots carrying a variety of weapons.

Bertram turned to the group behind him.

"Congratulations, posse, you have helped in the capture of Albert the Platypus, infamous bushranger and murderer of the brave Captain O'Hanlin."

The group gave themselves a short round of applause. It was at that point that Albert noticed both Bertram and Theodore were wearing badges on their vests. Theodore pointed at Albert.

"Some of you go down there and chain him up. Be careful—he is known to carry a pistol in his coat pocket."

There was quite a bit of milling about, but no one seemed eager to get down in the gully with Albert. Finally, Theodore jumped into the gully and hit Albert with the butt of his shotgun. After that, the rest of the posse was more than happy to run down into the gully and help subdue the already subdued platypus. In a few minutes, they had taken his pistol, his blanket, and his canteen. When they were finished, Albert had shackles on his paws and feet, a swollen eye, and a ripped jacket.

Theodore led the crowd out of the gully and onto the road. Albert shuffled along in the middle of the crowd as best he could. The chain on his leg shackles was very short and only allowed him to take small steps. Soon the entire group was spread out up and down the road.

The posse mocked him from a distance, still afraid to get too close. Theodore, though, remained close and hissed at Albert or poked him with his shotgun to move him along. Albert noticed a puckered wound on the side of Theodore's head. It was still healing.

Bertram caught up with Albert on the road and saw him looking at Theodore's wound.

"It can be very difficult sometimes to tell if Theodore is dead or not—after all, he is a possum. That said, your foreign friend came closer than most."

Bertram slowed his pace and walked alongside Albert down the middle of the road. He spoke softly so his voice wouldn't carry to the posse. "I must say that at the time I was very upset. What with poor Theodore all bloody, and tables knocked over. Even the dingoes were upset. With you and your friend gone, they had to make do with canned goods. All in all, it was not an anniversary party I would care to repeat."

Albert continued to shuffle down the road. The shackles kept tripping him, and he was more interested in keeping his feet than he was in listening to Bertram.

"However, in the end everything worked out for the best. I got to be the constable of Barton Springs and, last night, Theodore got to shoot your friend in the back."

Albert jerked his head toward Bertram.

Bertram smiled. "I thought that might get your attention."

"Is he dead?" Albert had been keeping quiet, afraid to give Bertram any information about his friends. There was no point in silence anymore.

"Probably. He left quite a blood trail behind. Theodore would have followed him, but the capture of the leader of the Platypus Gang was our first priority. Once we get you safely locked up, Theodore will go find the body."

Bertram drifted away to shake hands with the members of the posse. There was much backslapping, and congratulations were exchanged all around. Runners went back and forth between the town and the posse. Small groups of marsupials began to line the road and occasionally one of the children would throw a rock at Albert.

The pace of the procession was dictated by how fast Albert could move in shackles, and even with Theodore's prodding the trip was a long one. As it got dark, torches were brought out from town and delivered to the posse. A small band, with "Barton Springs Drum and Bugle Corp" printed on the bass drum, was waiting on the edge of town. It joined the procession playing marches and bugle solos.

The main street of Barton Springs was lined with spectators who cheered as the first posse members in the torchlight parade passed them. The cheers changed to boos and catcalls as the chained platypus got closer. Small children waved effigies of Albert with a noose around his neck as their parents looked proudly on. A banner had been strung across Main Street that read:

HURRAH FOR CONSTABLE
BERTRAM AND HIS BRAVE DEPUTY

You Saved Our Town

17

The Wages of Sin

At one time the jail had been an open shed, so there was no wall on the north side. The other three sides were made of uneven planks with enough gaps in them to allow blowing dust to cover the floor. The shingles on the roof had shrunk over the years and would have leaked if it ever happened to rain in Barton Springs. Two strap iron cages had been constructed inside the shed to hold the prisoners.

Roger and Alvin shared one of the cages with a scruffy tiger cat who was doing thirty days for vagrancy. Albert had the second cage to himself.

The tiger cat had tried to strike up a conversation with Albert the night he was brought in by the posse, but Roger and Alvin had sat in the corner of their cage and kept silent. By the next morning, the bandicoots still hadn't spoken a word to Albert.

Albert asked the bandicoots what had happened, but they refused to talk to him. Roger continued to sit in the corner of his cage, but by now he was holding his knees to keep his paws from shaking. Every so often he would mutter to himself that TJ had it coming. Alvin kept telling Roger that it was going to be all right and refused to look Albert in the eye.

Neither Bertram nor Theodore had reappeared after the

night they had caught Albert in the gully outside of town. Albert assumed they were looking for TJ, and each day they didn't come back gave him hope that TJ was still alive.

The first day in the cage was a never-ending parade of local inhabitants coming by the shed to stare at Albert the Platypus, a nonmarsupial and soon-to-be-hanged bushranger. Most were content to look at Albert from a distance and whisper among themselves. Some of the less timid would approach close to the cage and make rude noises at Albert. If he made any movement they would back away quickly and return only after he remained still. That day in Barton Springs was the first time in his life that Albert admitted to himself there might be worse places in the world than the zoo in Adelaide.

In the evening two armed kangaroos would escort a small wallaby to the jail. While the wallaby was putting food in the cages and emptying the slop buckets, the kangaroos would describe in detail the fate that awaited Albert at the end of a noose. He was going to be the first platypus hanged in Barton Springs. The novelty of the event didn't excite Albert as much as it did the kangaroos.

The next day was quieter than the first. Scattered groups of the curious visited the jail, but after one or two looks they would pass on down the street. Albert spent the morning sitting on the floor, ignoring the visitors and watching dust particles suspended in the beams of light that came from the holes in the roof. The particles stirred with each movement of the air in the cell, and if the breeze was gentle enough, the dust would create strange images in the columns of light. Albert couldn't see anything he recognized in the images, but concentrating on them took him away from the cell for a time and made the pain of knowing that TJ was dead or badly hurt a little easier to bear.

The noise of a soft cough broke Albert's concentration, and he looked up to see a wallaby standing in front of his cage. The wallaby was holding the paws of two very small wallabies. Albert looked again.

"Is that you, Ralph?"

The wallaby gave Albert a brief nod of the head. "I'm so glad you recognized me. It will mean so much to the children. Bernice. Jason. I'd like you to meet Albert the Platypus, famous bushranger and vicious killer."

The two little wallabies opened their eyes a little wider and one of them ducked behind its father.

"The wife really didn't like the idea of me bringing the twins. But I told her it would be a good object lesson, you know, the wages of sin and all that."

Albert didn't quite know how to respond. In all those years in Adelaide no one had ever introduced him to their children. He stood up in the cage. The second little wallaby also ducked behind its father.

"Pleased to meet you," Albert said quietly, not wanting to alarm the little wallabies any further.

Bernice and Jason poked their heads from around their father's back but refused to get any closer to the cage.

"I'm sorry, Albert, but they seem to be a little shy. You don't mind me calling you Albert, do you?" Ralph said hopefully.

"That's fine, Ralph. I don't mind a bit," Albert said, and immediately regretted it. Emboldened by familiarity, the wallaby began speaking to Albert sternly.

"On some levels you seem like a decent sort, Albert. I guess there is a little good in the worst of us. But one can't have platypuses rampaging around stealing and killing. If it weren't for the bravery of Constable Bertram and Deputy Constable Theodore, there is no telling how much damage you and your gang might have done."

Bertram had mentioned to the posse that Albert had killed O'Hanlin. Now here were more claims of involvement in the death of others being laid at his feet.

"What makes you think that I've been rampaging around stealing and killing?" Albert asked.

"As you are well aware, I know about your stealing first-hand," Ralph said, becoming a little petulant. "As to your murderous conduct, it has been the subject of numerous editorials and headlines in the *Gates of Hell Gazette*."

Ralph pulled a folded newspaper from inside his vest.

"The whole story is really quite chilling. Right here in last week's edition, it details how you and your gang came upon the Ponsby Station Fusiliers and murdered all of them in their sleep. You should be ashamed of yourself."

"We didn't do it, Ralph," Albert said in a pointless attempt to defend himself.

"Of course you did, Albert. It says so right here in the paper, and there was even worse to come."

Ralph turned a page in the newspaper and pointed to another article. "In this column it clearly says that a confidential source informed the editors of the paper of your plans to attack Barton Springs and subject the inhabitants to unspeakable cruelties."

He refolded the newspaper and put it back in his vest. "The town was able to hire Constable Bertram and his deputy to protect us, and as you know, they have done an admirable job."

Ralph took the paws of his children. "I must really get home. The hanging is sure to draw a crowd, and the wife and I are thinking about renting out the back room. Children, say good-bye to Albert."

The little wallabies shook their heads.

"Are you sure? There won't be a next time."

Bernice and Jason were sure. Ralph looked up.

"I guess not. Good-bye, Albert."

Albert lifted a paw and gave Ralph a wave. "Take care, Ralph."

The wallaby led his children away from the jail and down the street. Albert watched them for a few moments, then started to sit down again. He heard a voice.

"That's just an expression, right?"

Albert looked over and saw the tiger cat standing in the cage next to him. The bandicoots were still huddled in the far corner of the same cage. Roger's condition was getting worse, and he had started scratching himself.

"I beg your pardon?"

Roger started making whistling noises in the back of his throat. The tiger cat walked to the corner of the cage and absentmindedly kicked Roger a few times until he stopped, then walked back to where he had been talking to Albert.

"The wages of sin . . . it's just an expression, isn't it?"

"As far as I know it is," Albert answered after a moment's thought.

"Too bad. I could have used the money." The tiger cat turned and headed back toward the corner of the cell, where Roger had started whistling again.

18

"We Didn't Have Any Choice"

The next morning the kangaroos that kept watch on the jail opened the other cage and let the tiger cat go. It wasn't clear to Albert if his sentence was up or if they were just tired of feeding him. In any case, the tiger cat seemed indifferent to his release and hung around for a while making small talk with the jailers. The tiger cat ignored the bandicoots, who continued to sleep in a pile in the corner of their cage. However, before he left, the tiger cat stopped by Albert's cage, shook his paw, and wished him well.

With the tiger cat released, the kangaroos wandered off to find breakfast and a shady spot, leaving Albert to sit in the silence of the early morning.

The kangaroos had been gone only a few minutes when Bertram and Theodore came down the street and stepped up into the shed near Albert's cage. Theodore was still wearing his goggles to protect his eyes from the light, and still carrying his shotgun.

Bertram looked at Albert and put a finger to his lips. "Shhhhh," he whispered.

Then he pulled a pint gin bottle out of his coat pocket and tiptoed over to the bandicoots' cage. Bertram then gently rapped the gin bottle against the bars of the cage. The bandicoots were up like a shot. Roger had his paws through the bars before Alvin cleared the center of the cage.

Bertram pulled the bottle away from the cage. Roger became more and more frantic, pushing his arms through the bars as far as he could and grabbing at the bottle that Bertram kept just out of reach. In a few moments, Bertram tired of the game and let Roger have the bottle. He turned back to Albert.

"Good morning, Albert. I hope you slept well."

Albert looked up at Bertram.

"No point in being impolite, Albert. After all, I caught you fair and square, with a little help from your friends." Bertram gestured over to the bandicoots, who were rapidly passing the bottle back and forth between them.

"How's the newspaper business?" Albert asked.

Bertram smiled. "So you've come across a copy of the *Gates of Hell Gazette*. Theodore and I are quite proud of it, aren't we, Theodore?"

The possum nodded and fingered the stock of his shotgun.

Alvin handed the bottle back to Roger and then whined at Bertram. "You promised to let us go, Bertram. You promised us."

"Don't worry, Alvin, I haven't forgotten. In fact, that's why Theodore and I are here. Aren't we, Theodore?"

Theodore nodded and looked over at Alvin. Saliva began to glisten in the corners of Theodore's mouth.

"We just need you to do one more thing before you get the reward money. We would like you to take a few friends of ours to the hideout of the Platypus Gang. You'll be back in plenty of time for the hanging."

Bertram pulled a key out of his coat pocket and started to unlock the door of the bandicoots' cage. When Bertram mentioned the hideout, Albert jumped up. Bertram looked over as he continued to unlock the door.

"It seems that your friend from California had more blood in him than we thought. Theodore lost his trail at the edge of Hell. If he made it across the flats, I'm sure he went back to your little valley. Roger and Alvin are going to show us where that is, aren't you?" Bertram opened the door of the cage.

Roger staggered out first, still scratching himself. "Too right we're going to show you. That bloody foreigner stole my gun."

Alvin called over to Albert as he followed Roger out of the cage. "We didn't have any choice, Albert. He took away Roger's gin and called us rodents."

"I'm sure that was very unpleasant," Bertram said, and dismissed the bandicoots with a wave. "Theodore, please take these material witnesses over to the bar and get them ready for their trip."

Theodore got behind the bandicoots and herded them into the street with the butt of his shotgun. Bertram took a cigar out of his vest pocket, bit the end off, and spit it into the street.

"Every cloud has a silver lining—did you know that, Albert?"

Albert wasn't in the mood to listen to Bertram talk about clouds. He had to think of some way to escape before Roger and Alvin could lead Theodore or the dingoes or both to the water hole. Albert had spent so much of his life in a cage that being in the jail in Barton Springs hadn't made him frantic. He had escaped from Adelaide, and with enough time he would probably find a way to escape from Barton Springs. There was the matter of the hanging, but he had been too worried about TJ to dwell on the fact that his time to escape was limited.

"Our first meeting, except for the money in your pack, was unfortunate. Our second meeting, however, has been extremely profitable and, if I may say so, personally rewarding. By the time I had written two editorials, I had been hired to protect Barton Springs and the price on your head had been raised to ten pounds. That kind of money tempts anyone. Ask your little friends." Bertram gestured toward the departing bandicoots with his cigar.

"Of course everyone knows that money is secondary to my sense of civic duty," he continued. "Just yesterday there was an editorial in the *Gazette* which extolled my selfless heroism in capturing the notorious Platypus Gang. According to the paper, there is even talk of running me for mayor of Barton Springs. I'm humbled by the thought."

Bertram took a match out of his pocket, struck it on the bars of Albert's cage, and lit his cigar.

"I don't care if that friend of yours dies in the desert, gets eaten by the dingoes, or runs back to where he came from. Theodore, however, holds a grudge."

He took a puff on his cigar and blew a small smoke ring through the bars of the cage. "By the way, Albert, the whole time I have been here you haven't summoned one demon." The match burned Bertram's fingers and he dropped it on the floor of the jail. "You must be losing your touch."

Bertram ground the smoking match out with his heel and walked away, leaving Albert alone in the shed.

All Albert could think about as he watched Bertram catch up with Theodore and the bandicoots was that TJ was badly hurt and needed him. He felt like throwing himself against the bars, but he had seen too many animals hurt themselves doing that in Adelaide. He had done it himself right after he was caught and had soon learned that fear and desperation didn't get you out of a cage.

Bertram had been right about one thing: the chance of a demon showing up was pretty slim. If anyone was going to get Albert out of the Barton Springs jail, it was going to have to be Albert. All he needed was a plan.

In Adelaide he had waited until someone forgot to latch his enclosure. There wasn't much chance of him being that lucky a second time. The only other time the door to his cage was open was when they brought him food. He could probably overpower the wallaby, but the two kangaroos were another story.

The only advantage of being the lone platypus in this part of Old Australia was that no one knew about his poison spurs. TJ and the bandicoots had seen him attack the dingo, but TJ had killed it before the poison had a chance to work. It was almost certain that one kangaroo would shoot him while he was poisoning the other, but with luck, he might be able to take the gun from the one he jumped and use it first.

If that was going to be his plan, someone was going to have to die. You can't poison someone halfway, and it's hard to shoot someone just a little bit. Albert had never wanted to kill anyone and didn't want to kill anyone now. He had suppressed the memories of poisoning the dog that killed his mother and had remembered it clearly only after the fight with the dingo.

TJ had saved Albert's life more than once, but that wasn't important. What was important was that TJ was Albert's friend, and Albert was more than willing to die trying to save his life. The question was whether Albert was willing to kill someone else in the process. Albert didn't really know. He had no good reason to hate the kangaroos and probably couldn't develop one before the time came to act.

He sat on the floor of his cage waiting for the evening meal and trying to think of other ways to escape. By midday nothing had come to him. If he wanted any chance of helping TJ, he had to try to escape that evening, regardless of the consequences to himself or his jailers.

Albert got up and moved the slop bucket to the far end of the cage. Retrieving the bucket would force the wallaby to clear the door to the cage and give Albert a clear shot at the closest kangaroo. It was going to be a near thing, and he was going to need a lot of luck. Albert had told the crowd in Ponsby Station that a platypus was the luckiest animal in the world, but after spending time in Old Australia, he was beginning to have his doubts.

He was pacing off the interior of the cage, trying to estimate the time it would take the wallaby to reach the slop bucket, when he heard a familiar voice from the street.

"So you're the leader of the Platypus Gang."

Albert looked up to see Jack standing in front of the shed.

"To tell the truth, I was expecting someone a little tougher-looking," Jack continued.

Albert rushed over to the side of his cage closest to the street. Jack looked over his shoulder. The kangaroo on the other side of the street was slouched in a chair with his hat pulled down over his eyes to keep out the midday sun.

"Sorry I didn't get here sooner. I don't walk as fast as I used to."

In the years Albert had spent in the zoo, he had never seen a friendly face through the bars of his cage. For a second, memories of the overwhelming loneliness of his time in Adelaide washed over him, and he was afraid to say anything just in case the figure in the slouch hat and the dirty drover's coat might disappear at the sound of his voice.

"Are you doing all right, Albert?" Jack asked.

Albert hesitated for a few seconds before he answered. "I'm doing fine, Jack, but I've got a friend that's in trouble."

Jack took off his hat with his right paw and knocked some of the dust off it by slapping it against his leg. "I guess that makes two of us." He put his hat back on. "I'll be back in a couple of hours. Don't go anyplace."

Jack walked away from the jail, and Albert noticed that he was dragging his left foot.

19

Good-bye to Barton Springs

B y the time Jack managed to pry open the lock on the cage, dense clouds of smoke and ash were whirling down the street in front of the shed. The shed was one of the first buildings to catch fire, and if Jack hadn't shown up with the crowbar when he did, Albert would have burned to death. The kangaroos had long since abandoned their post, and the other creatures were too busy fleeing the fire to pay attention to what Jack and Albert were doing.

Jack wasn't able to use his left paw and had kept it in his coat pocket. As a result, Jack had some difficulty prying open the lock, but with Albert's help he had managed to open the cage with a minute to spare.

Albert had jumped into the street and had just helped Jack down from the shed floor when part of the roof collapsed, causing more sparks and debris to shoot skyward. Albert's hat and canvas jacket protected him from most of the sparks, but he did have to brush off one or two small pieces of smoldering wood before they burned through his clothes. Jack had brought a couple of bandanas with him, and Albert tied one over his face and helped Jack tie the other over his.

They pushed their way through the smoke and the constantly

changing wind until they came to the main street, where they joined small groups of refugees heading north out of the burning town. If any of the wallabies or bandicoots dragging children or pushing wheelbarrows full of salvaged housewares recognized Albert, they gave no sign.

Buildings on both sides of the street were on fire, and the banner that had once spanned the street had become ash that floated above the heads of the dispossessed. A few members of one of the bucket brigades along the street continued throwing water, not wanting to admit it was a pointless task. But others had abandoned their buckets and were trying to get possessions out of still-standing houses before the flames reached them.

Barton Springs wasn't a very large place, and Albert and Jack reached the edge of town ten minutes after leaving the jail. Those inhabitants that had already gotten out had stopped on the road, not knowing where to go next. They milled around the outskirts of Barton Springs, watching the fires and looking for friends to compare tragedies with.

Albert and Jack continued to walk north as rapidly as they could, and even with Jack's limp they soon left the inhabitants of Barton Springs behind them.

"I didn't expect the wind to come up like that," Jack said as he pulled the bandana down around his neck.

Albert pulled down his bandana. "Where are we going?"

"I stowed some gear in the hills close to the road."

Jack limped up the road, stopping every so often to look back at the smoke rising from Barton Springs. Albert wasn't sure what had happened to Jack or how badly hurt he was, so he kept Jack in front of him, just in case he needed help.

As they walked, Albert told Jack about TJ, the bandicoots, and how Bertram and Theodore were in league with the dingoes. Jack said he'd heard of Bertram and Theodore before and told Albert that they had a bad reputation in Old Australia. The word was that the possum had killed a couple of miners in a not-so-fair fight.

The trip between the town and the hills took less time than Albert's walk to Barton Springs in shackles, but it was dusk when Jack turned off the road. He pulled a small pack out of the brush and passed it to Albert.

"When I read about the hanging, I wasn't sure what I was going to find in Barton Springs. There is food, water, and a blanket for you in the pack."

Then he reached in the pocket of his coat and pulled out his old pepperbox pistol and held it out to Albert. "I didn't have time to get another gun, so take this one."

Albert hesitated. "I don't know, Jack. You might need it."

"Look, Albert, if I were going with you I'd keep it. But you don't have time to drag a cripple across the flats, not if you want to help that friend of yours."

Albert reluctantly took the gun. "What happened to you, Jack?"

"I'm not really sure. One minute I was walking up a hill, the next minute I was lying at the bottom of the hill with a bum leg and an arm that didn't work right. Scared the hell out of me." Jack pulled the other pack out of the bush. "Took me a week before I could get around much."

Albert didn't know what to do. Both TJ and Jack were hurt, but he couldn't be in two places at once. He knew that Jack was able to get around without him and that TJ was probably badly hurt somewhere between here and the water hole. The choice was simple, but it didn't make Albert feel any better.

"Wait here for me, Jack. I'll be back in a day or two."

Jack shook his head. "You don't know that for sure."

"Not for sure, Jack."

"I'll tell you what, Albert. If you get clear, meet me at Ponsby Station. I'll be set up near where the store used to be."

"I'm not sure that's a good idea—not after our last trip," Albert said.

"The place is pretty much deserted. They closed down the mine after O'Hanlin got himself and half the town killed."

Jack started to put on his pack, but he struggled with it as he tried to get the straps over his bad arm. Albert put the pistol in his coat pocket and helped Jack with his pack.

"It wasn't you, was it?" Jack asked.

Albert picked up his own pack. "It wasn't me what?"

"It wasn't you that killed O'Hanlin, was it?"

Albert shook his head. "Dingoes got him."

"I'm glad to hear it. I kind of liked O'Hanlin."

Jack looked over in the direction of Barton Springs. A soft glow from the burning town haloed the hills. "I think I'll wander back a little ways and watch the fire." He hesitated a few seconds, then went on. "That friend of yours is probably already dead. Don't get yourself killed over something you can't do anything about."

"I'll try not to, Jack."

Jack hobbled away toward the road. Albert shouldered his pack and walked into the hills toward the flats of Hell. It was some time before he realized that he had forgotten to tell Jack what he had learned about the Famous Muldoon.

20

"They Ate Alvin"

There was no moon that night and Albert had fallen twice, once into an unseen gully and once into the bed of a dry creek. Each fall had disoriented him a little bit more, and soon one star began to look much like the next and he lost all sense of direction. Desperate to find TJ, Albert had kept walking longer than he should have.

Finally, he stopped at the base of a small hill. There was a good chance that he was getting farther away from the water hole, not closer to it. He was going to have to wait until first light to start again.

Albert took a canteen and a blanket out of the pack Jack had given him and prepared to sit out the night. Continuing to travel blindly through the night would be the same as throwing himself against the bars of a cage. He took a drink from the canteen and pulled the blanket over his shoulders. Then he leaned against the rock and sat there for the rest of the night, alert for any noise or for the smell of dingoes.

The distant mountain appeared on the horizon in the faint light of morning, and Albert knew generally where he was. He would need to walk west.

Getting lost the night before had taken Albert far enough out of his way that he didn't reach the foothills until midmorning. He had tried to veer north toward where the cliffs began, but he miscalculated the angle and missed them by a few miles. He hurried past the hills and got to the trail that led up the cliff about an hour later. He stopped at the bottom of the trail and listened.

Albert couldn't hear anything, but the air smelled faintly of dingo. He took the pistol out of his pocket and started cautiously up the trail. He reached the top and continued into the gap in the cliff walls, stopping to listen every few yards.

He had stepped out of the gap and onto the trail leading down to the valley when he found the body of a dingo. There was a flint-tipped spear by the body, which had been spattered with red ochre.

He walked carefully down the trail to the campsite. The lean-to was still standing, and TJ's coat was lying on the ground under the canvas. Albert picked up the coat. It was stiff with dried blood and had a bullet hole in the back. He held TJ's coat for a few moments before folding it neatly and putting it back where he found it. Albert held his paw over the fire pit. The ashes were still warm.

Albert took out his pistol again and began to search the valley. He came upon another dead dingo lying half-submerged in the water hole. The body had been there for a while and the crayfish were beginning to feed on it. He walked the entire perimeter of the water hole but found nothing else.

Near the base of one of the cabbage palms, Albert found a set of bloodstained overalls that had been thrown on a bush next to the tree. The overalls belonged to one of the bandicoots, he couldn't say which.

He walked up to the spring above the water hole and found a third dingo lying at the base of the path that led up to the rock shelter. Except for a blind eye and a small puncture wound on his nose, the dingo showed no signs of injury. The trail up to the shelter was spattered with blood.

Finally, he climbed the trail and crawled into the shallow cave.

The brown snake lay dead near the entrance to the shelter. Its head had been crushed, and someone had scattered red ochre over its body. Spent percussion caps were scattered around a pool of dried blood that had been smeared across the floor of the cave. Albert searched the back and sides of the shelter, but found nothing else.

He spent the rest of the afternoon searching the valley for signs of TJ, but found none. Once or twice he thought he saw movement at the end of the valley, but dismissed it as just reeds swaying in the slight breeze that rippled the pond.

After convincing himself that it was futile to search further, Albert walked back to the water hole and sat on the bank, staring into his own reflection. He knew that TJ had returned to the valley. His bloody coat was proof of that. There had been a fight and someone, probably TJ, had killed the dingoes. Other than that he knew nothing for sure. Albert stayed there trying to put the pieces together until darkness covered the pond and only then walked back to the camp.

A few sticks of firewood remained near the fire pit, and Albert started a small fire with the matches he knew would be in the pack Jack had given him. There were tins of sardines there also, but Albert couldn't eat.

There was a chance the fire might attract attention. But Albert hadn't seen any sign of the living in his search of the valley, and he knew the cliffs around him prevented the light from reaching the flats below the water hole.

Albert sat and stared into the fire in much the same way as

he had stared into the water hole. He wasn't sure that TJ was still alive—and if TJ was alive, he wasn't sure where to start looking for him.

The fire had been reduced to embers when Albert heard a noise in the darkness beyond the camp. He put his paw on the pistol in his pocket. The wind was behind him, so he couldn't smell anything. He sat quietly, waiting for another sound. When the wind shifted direction, he smelled stale gin.

A pair of eyes, reflecting the embers of the fire, appeared in the night across from where Albert was sitting.

"They ate Alvin." Roger's voice was a hoarse whisper.

Albert took his paw off the pistol. "Where's TJ?"

"He screamed something awful."

Albert could hear Roger scratching himself.

"You wouldn't have a drink, would you, Albert?"

"No."

"You're not going to kill me, are you, Albert?" The eyes across the fire pit blinked several times.

"I thought about it."

"I saved his head." Roger's voice was becoming a whisper.

"Whose head, Roger?"

"Alvin's, of course, but don't worry, Albert. I have it in a safe place."

Albert moved slightly, and the eyes backed away from the campfire.

"I won't hurt you, Roger. I just need to know what happened to TJ."

After a moment the eyes came a little closer.

"I don't remember, Albert. It was a long time ago."

"It was yesterday, Roger."

"Was it?" The sound of Roger scratching himself intensified.

"The dingoes were yelling and howling, and Theodore was hissing and shooting up at the cave. I remember that."

Roger went quiet. Albert started to reach toward his pack, and again Roger backed away.

"I have some food in my pack, Roger. Do you want some?"

Roger giggled. "Alvin and I have plenty of crayfish. I put a dingo in the pond to feed them."

Albert kept talking to Roger in an even tone, afraid that any change of pitch in his voice might send Roger back into the darkness. "I really need to know what happened to TJ. Try to remember."

"The dingoes took him. I told you that already." Roger sounded annoyed.

"Sorry, Roger, I must have forgotten. Where did they take him?"

"Bertram and Theodore were very angry."

Roger came closer to the fire pit. Albert could almost see his outline.

"Bertram is not very nice. Did you know that, Albert?" Roger started whispering again.

"I know that, Roger."

"When the dingoes took TJ out of the valley, Bertram started hitting Alvin. It wasn't Alvin's fault the dingoes wouldn't let Theodore kill TJ, was it?"

It took an effort for Albert to keep his voice from showing what he felt. "I'm sure it wasn't."

"He was afraid to hit the dingoes, so he hit Alvin. That wasn't nice, was it?"

"No, Roger. It wasn't nice."

"He took away my gin before he left. That wasn't nice, either." Roger scratched himself a few times.

Albert didn't say anything, and Roger continued scratching.

"Alvin keeps asking me why they killed him instead of me and I don't know what to tell him," Roger said, beginning to worry. "What should I tell him, Albert?"

"I don't know, Roger. I really don't know," Albert said honestly.

"They didn't like the way I smelled," Roger said after a moment.

"Who didn't like the way you smelled?"

"The dingoes. That's why they ate Alvin. I told you that." Roger started getting annoyed again.

"I'm sorry."

"They smelled both of us and then they started killing Alvin. After a while they ate most of him and then they went away." Roger continued to fluctuate between confusion and reality. "Did you hear that, Albert?"

Albert listened carefully but heard nothing except a light wind moving the branches of an acacia. "I don't hear anything."

Roger shuffled his feet in the darkness. "It's Alvin screaming—can't you hear it?"

"It's just the wind, Roger."

The pupils of Roger's eyes darted back and forth. "Alvin needs me. I have to go."

"I can take you back to Ponsby Station." Albert didn't know what else to say.

"We like it here, me and Alvin." Roger blinked twice before he closed his eyes and disappeared.

Albert didn't sleep much that night, glad that TJ hadn't died in the cave yesterday and worried that Roger might reappear with Alvin's head.

At first light, Albert went and found Alvin's bloody overalls and burned them in the fire pit with some leaves from a eucalyptus he had discovered near the spring. He hoped there might be some magic in the gesture that would ease Roger's pain. Albert knew that one could never be sure about magic, but a lack of certainty is never a good reason to do nothing. Albert shouldered his pack and left the water hole while the smoke was still rising from the campsite.

21

A Circus Tent

Three of them were standing near a grevillea bush seventy yards up the shallow ravine from where he was standing. Albert had never been this close to a live dingo in the daylight, and it wasn't an experience he had been looking forward to.

One of them was carrying a short flintlock musket; the other two were armed with spears and clubs. Other than woven bags suspended from their shoulders, the dingoes were naked. Their foxlike faces were covered with a reddish fur and showed the scars of past fights. The one with the musket was older than the other two, and the fur on his muzzle was turning white.

Not so long ago Albert had assumed that fur was all anybody needed for modesty and had been insulted when Jack had mentioned he was naked. Now, the lack of clothing on the dingoes struck him as primitive. Old Australia had changed Albert in many ways, some for the better and some for the worse. Albert hoped that someday he would have the time to sort out which was which.

Albert had been glad to leave the valley. It had served its purpose in sheltering him and TJ when they were running from the Gates of Hell. Now it was just a place haunted by the dead.

He had gotten onto the flats and started walking toward the

center of Hell itself. He had only a vague plan. He needed to find TJ and avoid a direct confrontation with the dingoes.

If he could locate TJ without being discovered, there was a chance he could find a way to help TJ escape and return with him to Ponsby Station. There were problems with the plan, and Albert knew it. If TJ was still alive, there was a good chance he was too badly hurt to travel. If that proved to be the case, Albert would deal with it when he had to.

His sense of smell had helped him more than once, and it stood by him that morning. He smelled dingoes from the moment he hit the flats. Albert tried to keep the wind in his face, and when he smelled dingoes, he would alter his course to the left or the right and continue walking.

But every attempt Albert made to continue in a straight line was met by the smell of dingoes on the wind or the reflection of light from what might be a gun barrel. After an hour of zigzagging deeper into the desert, the wind stopped completely. Albert stopped with it, afraid to move without some sense of what might lie ahead of him. The wind remained still, and finally he decided to try to find cover and a place to rest. Unfortunately for him, he picked the wrong ravine.

Albert's train of thought was broken when one of the dingoes made a series of yipping sounds, ran down the ravine, and threw a spear at him.

He spun sideways, and the spear glanced off the back of his pack. He turned back toward the dingo, who was racing after the spear and transferring a club to his right paw. Albert managed to jerk Jack's pistol clear of his pocket and pull the trigger before the dingo reached him.

Thirty grains of black powder blew gold dust and pieces of iron pyrites into the face of the oncoming dingo.

The dingo staggered back but didn't fall. He had been blinded by the shot, and his face was a mask of blood and gold. The dingo began moving forward again, yipping and howling and trying to use his club on an enemy he couldn't see.

Albert backed away from the wounded dingo, who kept swinging his club in wide arcs around his body and hitting nothing but air. The two dingoes at the end of the ravine watched quietly as their companion swung his club until he was exhausted. Finally, the blind dingo let the club hang at his side, then stuck his bloody muzzle in the air and let out a plaintive howl. The older dingo walked a few yards toward the wounded one and shot him with his flintlock.

The living dingoes made no attempt to move closer to Albert, and the one firearm they had was now empty. Albert wasn't sure what to do next. Running was out of the question, and trying to kill the other two dingoes with gold dust was not realistic. Albert put the pistol back in his pocket. The spear that the dingo had thrown was on the ground near his feet.

At first Albert thought about grabbing the spear to defend himself, but then he remembered the body of the dingo he had found at the top of the trail to the valley. Acting more on instinct than reason, Albert picked up the spear and walked slowly over to the body lying in the middle of the ravine. The two other dingoes stood quietly as Albert laid the spear down next to the dingo sprawled in the dirt in front of him and then backed up a few yards.

Albert and the dingoes watched each other for a few moments. The older dingo handed his companion his musket and walked over to the body. He reached in his shoulder bag and took out a small leather pouch. The dingo opened the pouch and scattered the red ochre it contained over the body of the slain. A moment later, the old dingo heard something and looked up the ravine. Albert followed his gaze and saw a bulky figure wearing purple tights standing where the ravine sloped back up to the desert floor.

The old dingo raised his paw toward the figure, then disappeared into the brush along the ravine, followed by the younger one. The figure in the tights looked at Albert for a second, then turned and walked away, disappearing over the lip of the ravine.

Albert wasn't quite sure what had happened, but for now, he was still alive. He walked up the ravine to where the purple-clad figure had disappeared. The desert at the top of the ravine was covered in bottlebrush and saltbush. Albert carefully wove his way through the brush until he saw the tops of gum trees growing above. He could smell water from the direction of the trees and headed that way.

The bush gave way to a series of rocky hills. At the base of the hills was a large water hole surrounded by wattle and gum trees. A circus tent stood under the sparse shade of one of the trees.

It was a small tent and had red-and-yellow stripes, just as TJ had described. A ragged pennant with the word *Champion* flew from the peak of the little tent. Over the years, the colors had faded and the canvas had been patched so many times it was difficult to determine if the stripes had originally been vertical or horizontal.

Muldoon sat on a three-legged stool in the shade of an awning that protected the front entrance of the tent from the sun. He had his paws on his knees, and his eyes were closed.

Albert approached the tent quietly. Muldoon made no movement but to cock his head, as if trying to hear a sound far away.

Albert didn't say anything. It was obvious that Muldoon did

not want to be disturbed, and good manners dictated that Albert wait for a better moment to try to strike up a conversation.

There had been a Tasmanian devil in the zoo in Adelaide, and once you had seen one, they stuck in your mind. The zoo had kept animals they considered dangerous in separate enclosures, but over the years Albert had seen the Tasmanian devil twice as they moved him in a portable cage to different places in the park. The devil hadn't been much bigger than Albert, but there was a fierceness about him that Albert had never seen in any of the other creatures in the zoo. He kept striking out at the keeper through the bars of his cage, and he didn't care how much it hurt, not if there was the slightest chance of inflicting injury on the object of his dislike.

Sometime in the past, Muldoon had been terribly burned. The fur on one side of his face had been replaced by wrinkled scar tissue that covered his eye socket and left him with a stub of an ear. One of the paws resting on a knee was badly scarred and had twisted as it healed. The fur on the other side of his face was now more gray than black.

Muldoon's purple tights had been patched more times than the tent, and bits of fur showed through the places where older repairs had given way. It seemed to Albert that everything about Muldoon was being held in the present by a few pieces of thread.

Muldoon finally opened his eyes and looked over at Albert. "When I first came here, I could close my eyes and hear the crowds cheering my name." He stood up and looked out on the desert. "It's harder for me to hear them now."

22

The Famous Muldoon

Albert had set up camp near the water hole some distance from Muldoon's tent. As TJ had said, the Tasmanian devil was a creature of few words. He had told Albert he was welcome to water and then went back inside his tent. That had been several hours ago, and Muldoon had not reappeared.

Albert had emptied his pack, and for the first time he had a chance to make a complete inventory of what Jack had put together. Along with TJ's coat, which Albert had brought with him from the valley, the pack contained two blankets, water, and some matches. Jack had also included some hard biscuits, several tins of sardines, and a half-pint of whiskey.

After his experience at Ponsby Station, Albert had given up hard liquor. But he knew TJ had a taste for it, and he was glad that Jack had included some.

Albert ate two of the biscuits but didn't open any of the sardines. He would hunt the lagoon in the morning. He knew that Muldoon liked sardines, and he was hoping to trade the ones he had for information about TJ. It was obvious that Muldoon knew much more about the dingoes than Albert did and might be in a position to help.

Darkness came without a sign of the Tasmanian devil. Albert laid out his blankets and started a small fire. He was sure that both Jack and TJ would disapprove of the fire as being a dangerous act in enemy territory, but Albert felt he could take the risk. Muldoon was close by and seemed to be on friendly terms with the dingoes. Besides, the dingoes knew where Albert was, and if they came looking they could find him, fire or no fire.

The hills blocked any view he might have had of the distant mountain, but he could see the stars beginning to appear. They were the same stars that appeared early when he watched the sky from the valley entrance not so long ago. He was glad to see them again.

Albert was just getting ready to put a few more sticks on his fire when Muldoon walked into the light carrying his wooden stool. He put the stool down across the fire from Albert and sat.

Muldoon had changed his clothes and was now wearing a dark peacoat and a watch cap. The coat was worn and missing a few buttons. The cap had been pulled over on the side of his head to cover the stub of his ear and mask some of the scars on the side of his forehead. Muldoon looked at Albert with his good eye.

"I'm Muldoon."

"I'm Albert." Albert sat down on his blankets.

The Tasmanian devil seemed hesitant, as if not knowing what to say next. After a moment he spoke again. "Do you need more blankets? I have a couple of spare ones in the tent."

Albert shook his head. "I'm fine, thanks. It looks like a warm night."

Muldoon sat and fidgeted for a minute. "You probably need to get some sleep. I guess I'll head back."

Muldoon stood up and made a show of picking up his stool. It was clear that Muldoon was either shy or unused to conversation and would need a little help to get comfortable.

"Would you like a drink?" Albert reached in his pack and took out the half-pint of whiskey. Albert had observed that almost any friendship in Old Australia required the offer of alcohol.

Muldoon gratefully replaced his stool by the fire and sat down again. He took the offered bottle with his good paw and, with some effort, extracted the cork with the burned one. He took a small drink and passed the bottle back to Albert.

"I guess you don't get much company," Albert said as he took the bottle and held it in his lap.

Muldoon thought a moment. "Dingoes, I get dingoes. But they don't talk much."

"I don't know anything about dingoes," Albert volunteered.

"Dingoes are pretty strange." Muldoon thought for a moment. "They like living out here."

He lapsed into silence. Albert passed the bottle back to him, and Muldoon took another drink.

"How long have you been out here?" Albert asked.

Muldoon held the bottle in his good paw for a few moments, then took another drink. "About eight years. I came out here to die, but it didn't work out."

He passed the bottle back to Albert, who once again held it in his lap.

"You don't drink?" Muldoon asked.

"No." Albert passed the whiskey back to Muldoon.

"Neither do the dingoes—they can't stand the smell of the stuff." Muldoon took a sip and stared into the small fire in front of him. The light was absorbed by his jacket and hat but was reflected by the scars on his face. There was a sadness about him that Albert had seen that morning at the circus tent, a sadness he could feel as he watched Muldoon across the fire.

The Tasmanian devil spoke again. "Nobody comes out here except the desperate."

Albert waited for a few moments for Muldoon to continue, but he remained silent. Finally, Albert spoke. "Do you remember TJ? You helped him get through here awhile back."

Muldoon nodded.

"The dingoes took him two days ago and I'm trying to find him. He's a friend of mine." Albert was relieved to finally be able to get directly to the point.

"What happened?" Muldoon started putting the cork back in the bottle with his bad paw.

"I don't know for sure—I wasn't there. But it looks like there was a fight up at the water hole you took him to. TJ shot some dingoes. He was hurt and got captured, but the dingoes wouldn't let Theodore and Bertram kill him." The words tumbled out of Albert in rapid succession.

"The possum and the one-eared wallaby; I know of them." Muldoon had become focused. "What happened after that?"

"The dingoes took TJ out here someplace, and I guess Bertram and Theodore headed back to the Gates of Hell. That's all I know." Albert stopped talking and waited for some response from Muldoon.

Muldoon stood up and absentmindedly put the whiskey bottle in the pocket of his peacoat. He started pacing up and down by the fire.

"You can never tell about dingoes. They do one thing one day and then something completely opposite the next. But one thing they like is a good fight and another is bravery. If a dingo dies well they leave him with his weapons and scatter red earth over the body."

"TJ was one to hold his own," Albert said with absolute certainty.

Muldoon nodded.

"What will they do with him?" Albert was starting to hope that TJ might still be alive.

"You said he was badly hurt?" Muldoon sat back down on his stool.

"Theodore shot him in the back."

Muldoon waited a few moments before continuing. "If he fought well at the water hole and he survives that bullet in his back, the dingoes might adopt him."

"They adopt other creatures?" The more Albert learned about the dingoes, the more strange they seemed.

"As far as I know, the last time they did it was eight years ago. But there's always a chance." Muldoon picked up a couple of sticks and fed them into the dying fire.

"What happened this morning?" Albert asked.

"You mean with the dingoes?"

"Yes."

"They'd never seen a platypus before. If the young one hadn't gotten so full of himself, they might have left you alone."

Albert sat up straight when he heard Muldoon say *platypus*. "I'm not the first platypus you've seen, am I?" It took every bit of self-control Albert had to keep himself from shouting.

"There was one in the zoo where I came from," Muldoon said matter-of-factly.

"But not here. You've never seen another platypus here." Albert was afraid he already knew the answer, but he had to ask.

Muldoon shook his head. "I've fought in every mining town

in the territory and walked this desert for eight years, and you're the only one I've seen." He paused a second before continuing, "I'm the only devil in Hell and you're the only platypus."

Muldoon fished the whiskey bottle out of his coat pocket and sat down on the wooden stool. He started to pull the cork and thought better of it, then tossed the bottle back to Albert. "You heard the stories, didn't you?" he asked.

"What stories?" Albert put the bottle in his pack.

"The stories about a place where nothing has changed and Australia was the place it once was."

Albert nodded. "That was what everyone talked about at the zoo in Adelaide."

Muldoon bent toward the dying fire. "Is this the place you expected to find?"

"No," Albert answered.

"When I first got here I thought there would be some of my kind in Old Australia." Muldoon stood up and used the side of his foot to push dirt over the embers of the fire. "Now I'm not sure anymore *what* my kind is."

23

Dingoes

Before sunrise the next morning, Muldoon appeared back at Albert's camp, carrying a walking staff and with several canteens looped over one shoulder. He was still wearing his watch cap, but the peacoat had been replaced by a stained cotton jacket that also had seen better days.

Muldoon told Albert he was going to try to find TJ, and he cautioned Albert to wait at the water hole until he returned. Then, without another word, Muldoon walked into the brush and was soon lost from sight.

Albert had wanted to give Muldoon the sardines before he left but had hesitated. He knew that once the sardines were brought out of the pack he would have to talk about Jack, and he wasn't quite ready to do that yet. He was pretty sure that one of Jack's fires had caused Muldoon's burns, and he was afraid that Jack might be such a sore point with Muldoon as to interfere with TJ's rescue.

The weather had been hot and the air so still that the pennant on top of Muldoon's tent stayed limp in the daylight hours. The water hole was cool in the early mornings, and Albert spent the time hunting grubs and freshwater shrimp. By midday, the sun heated the shallow water to an uncomfortable level, and the little creatures that lived in the water hole went into hiding in the mud and rocks that lined the bottom.

Albert spent his afternoons lying in the shade of a blanket that he had suspended between two gum trees a few yards from the water. He would lie on his back with his head supported by his pack, close his eyes, and try to imagine what the world he was looking for would be like. It would have other platypuses in it. That was for sure. But he wasn't certain what else that world might contain. His past visions of cool water and shady riverbanks hadn't survived his time in Old Australia.

Dozing in the heat of those afternoons, Albert would sometimes dream that the place he was looking for would be just another zoo without bars, and the banks of any river he found would be lined with unfriendly platypuses eating cotton candy and throwing rocks.

The noise of small black flies buzzing around his face would get louder, and he would pull himself back from the dream and into the shade of his blanket. He would lie there trying to brush away the flies and worrying that TJ might be a long time dead.

The water hole became a magical place in the brief dusk between the heat of the day and the cold of the desert night. Albert would walk in the fading light around the water hole to Muldoon's tent and look at the red-and-yellow patches that covered the tent. If he was in luck, a small breeze might straighten the pennant for a moment, and the word *Champion* would flutter above the tent.

Albert wondered what the tent might contain, and what it might have looked like when Muldoon was still a champion and its stripes were new. The tent and Muldoon had become one in Albert's mind, their current shabbiness making their past glories seem grander than they might really have been.

As much as Albert wanted to know what was inside the tent, he made no attempt to go inside or to peek through the drawn curtains that covered the entrance. It would be Muldoon's life he was walking into, and one didn't do that sort of thing without an invitation—and an understanding that you never walked into someone's life without being changed by the experience.

Albert would stare at the tent for a while and try to imagine the crowds yelling Muldoon's name, but he had never seen Muldoon fight, and his imagination wasn't up to creating an entire world of mining camps and blood sports. All that came to mind was the Muldoon he knew: the one covered in scars, waiting for the cheers that he knew would never come again.

Then Albert would walk away from the tent, collect his blanket and his pack from the bushes, go back to his camp, and start a small fire. He would wrap himself in the blanket and lean against his pack. If he was still hungry, he would eat a biscuit or two and then watch the fire until he fell asleep.

Five days after Muldoon left to look for TJ, Albert woke up to find an old dingo watching him from the edge of the brush near his camp. Albert wasn't certain, but he was pretty sure the dingo was the same animal he had encountered in the ravine nearby.

The dingo was squatting in the open across the coals from where Albert had fallen asleep. He had his flintlock musket in one paw and what looked like TJ's hat in the other. Albert sat up slowly and shrugged the blanket off his shoulders. He and the dingo watched one another for several minutes, neither making any sudden movements.

The old dingo got slowly to his feet and walked toward Albert. When he had covered half the distance, he put the hat on the ground and then backed his way to his original position. The dingo squatted again and waited.

Albert, following the dingo's lead, got up slowly, walked over, and retrieved the hat, then returned to his blanket and sat down. He looked down at the hat in his lap. It was TJ's hat, chinstrap and all. Albert raised his paw to the old dingo. The dingo raised his paw in return and stood up. He turned back toward the brush and beckoned for Albert to follow him.

Muldoon had told Albert to wait for him, but that had been several days ago. If the dingo was the same one from before, Muldoon had been on good terms with it—and so far, the dingo had been acting more like a friend than an enemy.

Albert had not forgotten that he had caused the death of a young dingo and that there was always the possibility that the old dingo's manner masked an elaborate plan for revenge. However, it was certain that the old dingo had some connection with TJ, and that was enough for Albert to take the risk.

He stood up slowly, took the canteen out of his pack, and went to the water hole and filled it. When he returned, the old dingo was still waiting for him.

Albert picked up his blanket and put it in the pack along with the canteen and his jacket. He left Jack's pistol in the coat pocket. It was going to be too hot to wear the coat, and the gun was almost useless. If the dingo meant him any harm, he would have to depend on the weapons nature had given him. He tied TJ's hat on the back of the pack, pulled the pack straps over his shoulders, and started toward the dingo.

When he was sure that Albert was behind him, the dingo trotted into the desert. Albert followed and found himself keeping up a pace he wasn't used to. The dingo moved effortlessly through the desert, and he seemed to know just when and where to go to keep from being slowed by clumps of brush or rough terrain.

The early morning air was cool, and Albert found that if he stayed close enough to the dingo in front of him, he could move along the desert floor with the same lack of effort.

But the dingo's smell was very strong, and at first Albert was repelled by it. It still reminded him of the killing of his mother, and that conjured up the zoo in Adelaide, and the horrors that had resulted from her death.

The longer the smell surrounded him, the less it bothered him. As an adolescent he had smelled the dog that killed his mother and that he had killed in turn. There was no subtlety in the memory of that smell from so long ago.

The scent of the dingo in front of him was different. The odor of dog was still there, but it was only a part of something more complex. The dingo smelled like wattle, like the red earth that covered the desert floor, like wood smoke, and like the distant smell of water and gum trees. The dog had smelled of domestication and slavery.

None of the things that Albert had thought were simple in Adelaide had remained that way in Old Australia. What he had thought was evil for so long was now helping him to save a friend.

The dingo slowed his pace with the coming of the midday heat. They kept walking for a while, but before the sun reached its zenith, the dingo led Albert to a rock outcropping that provided enough shade to offer them some relief.

The dingo leaned his musket up against one of the rocks and took a pawful of dried beetles from his woven bag, ate some, and gave some to Albert. In turn, Albert took his canteen out of his pack and passed it to the dingo. The dingo wouldn't drink directly out of the canteen, but would pour a little water in a paw and lap it into his mouth.

After they finished eating the beetles, the old dingo curled up in the shade and closed his eyes. Albert prepared to wait out the heat with his new companion.

The stillness of the desert was broken by the whisper of a dry wind that came up almost as soon as they had reached the shelter of the rocks. The wind was strong enough to keep the flies away, and Albert was grateful for it. The dingo lay still, his short fur occasionally ruffled by the moving air that found its way between the stones around them. Occasionally, he would flick an ear to the left or the right, as if trying to identify a distant sound, or he would raise his head, smell the wind, then settle back and close his eyes again.

Albert had known nothing of the desert when he first came to Old Australia. He had learned what he knew from Jack and his own trips across the flats of Hell. The morning he had spent trotting after the dingo had taught him a little bit more, but Albert knew it wasn't enough and never would be. The dingo sleeping near him was at home here. It was where he belonged.

Albert knew that he belonged someplace else. Where that place was, he didn't know, but it was somewhere, and as soon as his friends were safe, he would look for it again.

A gentle tap on the shoulder roused him from a light sleep. He opened his eyes to see the old dingo standing in front of him. The sun was getting low on the horizon, and the dry wind was cooler than it had been before. The dingo trotted back into the desert. Albert struggled to put on his pack and hurried after him.

The nature of the desert had changed that afternoon. Albert and the dingo trotted out of the flats onto a finger of red sandstone that extended into the desert from a low-lying rock ridge a mile or so ahead of them. Albert could see small columns of smoke rising from somewhere beyond the ridge.

They walked slowly up the finger of rock for an hour, and it was nearly sunset when they reached the top of the ridge. Below them, a small dingo encampment was scattered across a small sandstone plateau. Near where they stood, a spring trickled clear water through the rocks and down onto the plateau. The water ran into small pools worn in the sandstone, overflowed them, then escaped over a lip of rock beyond the camp.

Small campfires were burning in front of simple brush shelters that had been built haphazardly across the plateau. Dingoes sat near the fires working on stone tools or cooking pieces of meat that Albert didn't recognize. A few dingo pups played an endless game of tag through the camp, and their yips of excitement were the only sounds Albert could hear.

Muldoon was standing in the middle of the camp, his burned paw in the jacket of his peacoat. He looked up on the ridge and waved to Albert with the paw that still worked.

24

Moonlight and Laundry

TJ lay on his stomach on a pile of cut grasses that had been placed on the floor of one of the brush shelters in the dingo encampment. He turned his head slightly when Albert crawled through the entrance.

"I should have known better than to trust a drunk."

It was dark in the shelter, and what light there was came from a campfire not far from the entrance. It took a few moments for Albert's eyes to adjust to the dim light.

Woven bandages had been wrapped around TJ's chest, and they held a poultice of leaves pressed up against the wound in his back. His bloody long johns and canvas pants lay folded at his feet, and next to them was the cotton sack holding the rest of his possessions. The Enfield carbine had been propped against the brush wall of the shelter, close enough for TJ to reach it. A bowl of water was sitting on the ground.

Albert sat up and his hat brushed the roof of the shelter. "How are you doing?"

"Better than I was a week ago." TJ propped his head on his paws and spoke in a low voice. "How about yourself?"

"A little tired." Albert crossed his legs and leaned forward so he could hear TJ better.

"What happened to the rodents?" TJ asked.

"Alvin's dead and Roger went crazy."

TJ closed his eyes. "Not much of a loss, if you ask me."

Albert shifted position and his shadow moved on the far wall of the shelter. "Maybe not, but they were good to me once."

TJ rolled onto his side. "I'm glad to see you, Albert."

"You, too, TJ. I wasn't sure you were alive."

TJ smiled. "If I'm not dead, it wasn't for a lack of trying to kill me."

"What happened in Barton Springs?" Albert asked.

"Not much to talk about. I found the general store. It was dark by then, and I thought it was safe enough. I'd started for the back door when I heard Roger call out to me. Before I could get three more steps, someone behind me fired a shot. I didn't even look back. I ran . . . I've run before, Albert, and I'm good at it."

"It was Theodore. He was the one who shot you." Albert took off his hat and shoved it into his jacket pocket.

TJ was quiet for a few moments. "I figured it might have been that damned possum when I saw him at the water hole. I'll make sure of him the next time." He reached out for the bowl of water and took a long drink. "Sorry I couldn't get back to you. I didn't realize how badly I was hit until I got to the edge of town."

"Don't worry, TJ. I got by." Albert reached out and gently took the bowl out of TJ's paw.

"It took me awhile, but I got back up to the water hole. I was going to wait for you in the valley, just like we said." TJ was getting tired and the pauses were becoming longer. "Two days after I got there, company showed up . . . It was a hell of a fight, Albert. You should have seen it."

Albert held out the water. TJ shook his head and continued.

"I shot the first dingo that came through the gap, and it

delayed the rest of them until I could get up to that cave of yours in the cliff. After that it got real exciting."

TJ stopped talking and rested for a few moments before he continued.

"Bertram never came within rifle shot or I would have tried for him. The possum would run in for a few shots and then run back out of range again. The dingoes were the ones that carried the fight. If I hadn't started bleeding again and I'd had a little more ammunition, me and that snake would have held that cave until hell froze over."

TJ closed his eyes again. "Funny thing about that snake. It crawled out from somewhere right after I got into the cave. It coiled up between me and the entrance and stayed there for the whole fight. I broke my wound open running up to the cave, and I had started losing a lot of blood. Late in the day I began blacking out. The last thing I remember was that snake striking at a dingo that was trying to get at me."

Albert had been saddened by the death of the snake when he had found its body at the mouth of the cave. He was glad the snake had died bravely, but that didn't make it any less dead. Albert would miss it.

"It was a good snake" was all he could think to say.

TJ opened his eyes briefly. "Would you do me a favor?"

"Of course I would."

"Would you wash the blood out of my clothes?" TJ closed his eyes. "I can't abide being dirty." TJ took a deep breath and fell asleep.

Albert gathered up TJ's pants and long red underwear and crawled out of the shelter with the clothes under one arm.

Muldoon was sitting by the fire outside the shelter. Albert's pack was sitting next to him. The moon was full and low enough in the night sky to light up the whole plateau. The other fires in the encampment were beginning to burn out, the dingoes mere shadows that moved from time to time among the other shelters.

Muldoon looked over at Albert, the moonlight softening the scars on his face. "How is he?"

Albert walked over to his pack and opened it. "He's sleeping."

Albert took TJ's coat out of his pack and put it with the rest of the bloody clothes he had taken from the shelter. TJ's hat hadn't suffered much, so Albert put it aside. As he started to close the pack, he remembered the sardines. He was going to have to talk to Muldoon about Jack sometime, and this might be as good a time as any.

Albert reached into the bottom of the pack and pulled out the tins of sardines. "I understand you like these."

Muldoon looked at the sardines in Albert's paw and then at his face. "Who told you that?"

"TJ, for one." Albert extended the sardines to Muldoon.

The Tasmanian devil hesitated, reached out slowly and touched the tins for a brief moment, then withdrew his paw without taking the sardines. Muldoon looked back into the fire and said nothing.

Albert held the sardines for a moment more, then laid them down on the ground next to Muldoon. He picked up TJ's clothes and walked to the stream coming down from the ridge. He followed the water past the pools to where it spilled over the sandstone escarpment and flowed into a grove of gum trees a hundred yards beyond the dingo camp. The dingoes got their water from the pools close to their shelters, and Albert didn't want TJ's blood mixing with their drinking water.

The moonlight was reflected by the water and the stones around him, and there was more than enough light for washing.

Albert wet the clothes, gently rubbed them on the sandstone, then rinsed them in the stream. When he finished, he stretched the wet clothes flat on the stones to await the next day's sun.

Albert sat at the edge of the plateau and looked over the tree-tops in the grove below him. The moon was beginning to move higher in the sky, and its light dimmed the stars around it.

For the first time since he had arrived in Old Australia, Albert felt at peace. There had been that brief two days between meeting Jack and the fire at Ponsby Station when no one was chasing him or creatures he knew weren't being shot at or eaten.

TJ was alive. Jack was waiting for him at Ponsby Station. The zoo in Adelaide was now ancient history, and Hell was proving to be a pretty good place.

Albert decided to spend the night by the stream where he could see the trees. He was just getting up to retrieve his blanket when he saw Muldoon walking toward him across the sandstone.

"They're afraid of you. Did you know that?"

"Who's afraid of me?"

"The dingoes."

Albert was always surprised by the idea that anyone could be afraid of him. It was true that the citizens of Barton Springs had kept their distance, but Albert had thought that was just the result of some bad press and hadn't taken it personally. "That doesn't make any sense."

"It does to them." Muldoon sat down next to Albert, using his good paw to ease himself onto the sandstone. "Your footprints started it, and then there was that business with the snake."

"My footprints?"

Muldoon shrugged. "How many other creatures run around out here with webbed feet? None, that's how many. The dingoes don't miss much. They've seen your tracks. They smell poison on you and they smelled poison on one of their dead. That cave where they got TJ had your footprints all over it, and when that snake killed another dingo, they began to put two and two together. Shooting one of them with gold dust just added to the legend. If I didn't know better, I might be afraid of you myself."

"I didn't think Tasmanian devils could be afraid of anything," Albert said after a moment of reflection.

Muldoon laughed. "Neither did I. Then I got famous and everything changed."

"What changed?"

Muldoon stopped laughing. "I became afraid of not being famous." He stood up slowly. "How's Jack?"

Albert hesitated. "Getting old," he finally said.

"I recognized his pistol when you fired that shot the other day." Muldoon looked down at Albert. "Are you going to see him again?"

Albert nodded. "I promised to meet him at Ponsby Station."

"Tell him I'll save the sardines until he gets here."

Muldoon made his way back toward the dingo camp, leaving Albert surrounded by moonlight and wet clothes.

25

A Platypus Unleashed

CALL TO ARMS!
VOLUNTEERS WANTED—
NEW REGIMENT FORMING

**All able-bodied marsupials wanted for
punitive expedition
Remember Ponsby Station!
Remember Brave Captain O'Hanlin!
Remember Barton Springs!
Civilization in jeopardy!
Dingoes and Platypuses—crimes against nature!
Report to Gates of Hell on or before June 1st next
Many medals available**

Signed: General Bertram, Commanding

Col. Theodore, in charge of ordnance

Albert tore the poster off the tree and put it in his pocket along with the reward posters he'd been saving. Every gum tree Albert had seen since he reached the hills near Ponsby Station had been plastered with handbills. Most were calls for volunteers; the rest were reward posters with his name on them. The price on his head was now up to twenty pounds. He was being blamed for killing O'Hanlin, burning down Barton Springs, and selling guns to non-marsupials. Albert wasn't quite sure what a punitive expedition was, but whatever it was, it was being directed at him and the dingoes.

It had taken only two days to get to Ponsby Station from the dingo camp. Muldoon had told Albert that most of the trails that led into Hell went through the lava flow, but there were shortcuts through the hills if one knew where to look for them.

A young dingo had led Albert to the edge of Hell and no farther. It had been a strange trip. The dingo would walk or trot ahead of Albert but wouldn't look at him. He would disappear at night only to reappear in the morning. When they reached the hills, the young dingo disappeared for the last time.

Albert was glad to be back on his own. His silent companion had made the trip across the flats much quicker, but it had also been a reminder of how deep the gulf was between the dingoes and himself.

Muldoon had told Albert that while TJ's fight at the water hole had been good enough for his possible adoption, the major reason the dingoes took TJ away from Bertram and Theodore was because of Albert.

His looks and actions had become the subject of much conjecture around the campfires. TJ and Muldoon had pointed noses and pointed ears, and the dingoes could understand bravery in creatures that looked much like themselves.

In Albert's case, it was unimportant to the dingoes whether he was brave or not. It was clear to them that there had to be some magic associated with him and the events that he played a part in. The dingoes had learned that trying to hurt a friend of Albert's could get you bitten by a snake and that trying to hurt Albert personally could get you a faceful of gold dust.

Dingoes weren't stupid. If they couldn't find a stranger to fight with, they were more than willing to fight among themselves, but they weren't suicidal. Albert was obviously too foreign or too dangerous to take lightly. Helping him or his friends was a cheap price to pay to stay on his good side. After reading the recruiting posters, Albert was afraid that the price might turn out to be more expensive than the dingoes had expected.

He reached the trail he had taken from Ponsby Station to the lava fields shortly before noon and turned south toward the settlement. The trail was familiar, and Albert was able to reach their old campsite by nightfall.

Albert made a cold camp that night, partially in memory of his and Jack's flight from the wreckage of the mercantile, but mostly because he was a wanted animal in Old Australia. He wrapped himself in a blanket and lay back against his pack, glad to be alive.

He tried to remember what he had been like when he first came to Old Australia, but that had been some time ago and the animal that had arrived in that dust storm was long gone. He had been replaced by an animal that carried a pack, slept under blankets, and had an unflattering description of himself posted on every tree in the territory. He could remember all the things that happened to him and all the things that he had learned, but in living those events he had become what he was, and the animal he had once been was now a stranger. He fell asleep dreaming of dust storms and singing wombats.

Before the sun showed itself over the hills, Albert had already begun walking down the trail to Ponsby Station. The holes that lined the gully leading into town were quiet. No whistles came from the empty burrows, and the flowers in the coffee cans at the entrances had died from lack of water.

The silence of the morning was broken by drunken laughter drifting up the gully from the center of town. Albert hurried down the trail and onto the flat piece of ground next to the mine.

The rock foundations of the mercantile were still standing, but the building itself had been completely destroyed by the fire. Someone had cleared the site. Piles of burned timber, broken glass, and rusted tin had been shoveled to one side of the rock footings. A construction scaffold was still standing at one corner of the foundation, and a few uprights and wooden beams had been put into place. Work on the building had stopped long enough ago for the uprights to become covered with posters and broadsides.

Jack was standing on the foundation under one of the beams with a rope around his neck. The rope had been thrown over one of the beams and then secured to one leg of the scaffold. Jack was trying to keep his balance, but his crippled leg was on the verge of collapsing.

Two kangaroos and a large wallaby were standing in front of Jack, laughing and drinking from half-pint bottles. One of the kangaroos had on a bowler hat and was wearing checked pants. The other kangaroo and the wallaby were roughly dressed and carried rifles in their free paws. Two grubby adolescent bandicoots were sitting on the footings on the other side of the foundation. They wore overalls and had on tweed caps.

In between drinks, the kangaroo in the bowler would demand that Jack tell them where Albert was. When Jack wouldn't answer, the kangaroo would slap him across the face and take another drink. With each slap, Jack would wobble on the footing and the noose on his neck would tighten. The noise from the blow would carry across what remained of O'Hanlin's store, and the eyes of the young bandicoots would widen at the sound. The last rational thought Albert had before he went berserk was that the kangaroo in the checked pants looked familiar.

The rage didn't spiral up from inside of him as it had done in the past. It was just there, and it was complete.

He felt his pack fall away and heard it hit the ground behind him. Ahead of him everything moved in slow motion. He could see the bandicoots point toward him and the kangaroos and the wallaby turn their heads. Albert looked down and saw small puffs of dust rise in the air with each footfall as he ran across the flat ground toward the mercantile. He looked up again and saw a cloud of smoke as the wallaby fired his rifle, and he heard the ball pass by his head.

Before another shot could be fired, Albert was in the air with his feet in front of him. He hit the kangaroo with the rifle and felt his spurs sink into its chest. As Albert fell backward, the other kangaroo struck him with a billy club.

The blow caught Albert on the shoulder, but he couldn't feel it. He could hear the kangaroo that he had just poisoned start to scream. The uninjured kangaroo bent over to try to hit him again. He kicked up as high as he could, and his spurs caught his attacker in the throat. The kangaroo looked surprised and dropped the club he was holding. He slowly sat down in the dirt, and the bowler hat slipped from his head and rolled a few feet away.

Albert jumped to his feet and ran at the wallaby, who was trying to put another paper cartridge in his rifle. The wallaby turned to run, and Albert jumped on his back and spurred him in the flanks. The wallaby carried him for a few feet, then fell on his face. Albert jumped up again and spun around. He and Jack were the only creatures still standing.

The young bandicoots had taken cover behind the foundation and were peeking at Albert over the stone footings. The kangaroo he had hit in the chest was still screaming. The wallaby was moaning and twitching in the dirt. The kangaroo in the checked pants was bent over and making a gurgling noise. One of Albert's spurs had caught him in the jugular, and blood was pouring down his front and over his pants.

Albert stood there, shaking his head, and tried to make some sense of what had just happened. The screaming bothered him a little bit. He remembered that the dog on the banks of the Murray had screamed after he had spurred it, and he wondered abstractly how badly it must hurt to be poisoned by a platypus. He looked over at the bowler in the dirt and recognized it. The bleeding kangaroo had been the bouncer at O'Hanlin's.

The screaming stopped, and the wallaby stopped twitching. The kangaroo in the checked pants finished bleeding to death, and everything came back into normal time. Albert's shoulder began to hurt. He walked over to Jack, took the noose from around his neck, and helped him sit down on the foundation. Jack didn't say anything but kept glancing at the bodies scattered around him.

The bandicoots made their way carefully around the foundation and stopped by the scaffolding. They stared at Albert for a moment and then whispered to each other. One of them reached up and tore down a reward poster from the upright on the corner. They looked at it and whispered some more. The one holding the poster started walking toward Albert but hesitated. His friend gave him a push.

The bandicoot came over and stood in front of Albert. He reached in the pocket of his overalls and took out a pencil stub. The bandicoot wiped his nose with his forearm and held the poster and the pencil up to Albert.

"My mate wants your autograph."

26

Good Intentions

Jack had set up the tripod and billycan with the use of one arm, and he'd gotten upset when Albert tried to help him. It was obvious to both of them that Jack's condition hadn't improved since Barton Springs, and it wasn't likely to in the future. Jack could still carry his pack and do the chores necessary to survive. But he was slow at it, and each time he struggled with something that had once been easy, he became irritated.

The cup was warm in Albert's paws, and the smell of the tea helped mask the odor of death that he had carried with him from Ponsby Station. It had been two days since they had left that place, and he and Jack had encountered nothing but open desert during that time.

Muldoon had told Albert that as soon as TJ was able, they would go back to Muldoon's camp by the water hole, and Albert and Jack were to meet them there. The word would be out among the dingoes to watch for them and guide them back across the flats of Hell.

No dingoes had appeared, and Jack and Albert had been on their own since they had come out of the hills. Each morning Albert would start walking toward the mountain on the far horizon. He knew that the camp he was looking for was between himself and there, but not much more.

When Albert had told Jack that Muldoon wanted to see him, Jack just said that he expected it to happen someday, and now was as good a time as any. They had moved slowly, not covering much distance each day. Albert was glad for the pace. It gave him time to think, and it gave the dingoes more time to find them. Jack moved ahead in a stoic fashion, favoring his bad leg and keeping quiet about what he expected out of his meeting with Muldoon.

They hadn't spoken about the killings at Ponsby Station. Jack had given Albert a gruff thanks and left it at that. Albert had returned the borrowed pistol and considered taking a gun from one of the dead, but thought better of it. What had happened there was done, and he wanted no souvenirs of the event.

Jack hobbled over from the tripod with the billycan and refilled Albert's cup. It was late afternoon, and they had stopped for the day in a grove of acacia. A breeze was coming out of the west. It was sufficient to cool the afternoon but not so strong as to kick up any dust. Albert sat leaning against his pack, sipping his tea and hoping the clear skies would hold through the night.

Jack returned the kettle to the tripod and moved away from the small fire to the sparse shade of a nearby acacia. He sat down in the shade, took a last drink from his cup, and threw the dregs into the bush behind him.

"So this is Hell."

"That's what the signs said." Albert looked up at the sky, but no clouds had appeared.

"Looks pretty much like everywhere else…Sardines?" Jack started digging in his pack.

"No thanks."

Jack found a can of sardines, opened it, and ate half the contents before speaking again.

"I looked for Muldoon, Albert. Did I tell you that?"

"No, Jack, you didn't."

Jack thought for a moment and then shook his head. "I could of sworn I said something about it." He went back to eating the sardines.

"Muldoon told me that he was afraid of not being famous," Albert said, trying to keep Jack talking.

Jack looked over at Albert and shrugged. "That's because fame was the only thing he ever had, except maybe me and a few cans of fish." He looked at the can he was holding in his good paw. "Muldoon came out of the desert looking for a place he heard about that didn't exist. He had to settle for being famous."

He got up and wandered into the bush, looking for a place to bury the sardine can. Then he spent a few minutes looking for snakes that might be hiding in the brush, but his heart didn't seem to be in the hunt, and he soon retreated to the shade of the acacia. Albert spent the rest of the afternoon lying against his pack, getting up only to collect firewood for the evening. Whatever thoughts they may have had they kept to themselves.

With the coming of darkness they built up the fire and waited for the dingoes to find them. The dingoes should have seen the fire the night before. If they didn't see it tonight, something had to be wrong. Albert was beginning to think he should have picked up a gun when he had the chance.

Jack hadn't said much about coming into Hell when Albert told him where they were heading. He had shrugged and said if it was a good enough place for Albert and Muldoon, it was a good enough place for him. He was a little more curious about the dingoes, whom he had only heard of in whispers. After Albert told Jack what he knew about the dingoes, Jack said that he was glad to hear they were friendly, but that he was going to reload his pistol with lead balls, just in case.

Albert was surprised at how quickly he had come to accept dingoes as a natural part of his world. Other than their eating habits, which took some getting used to, the dingoes were straight-up creatures. They had proven to be brave and loyal, which was more than he could say for most of the other inhabitants of Old Australia.

Muldoon had told Albert that the dingoes never left the flats of Hell. If someone was imprudent enough to come to where they lived, the dingoes ate them and that was the end of it. They made exceptions to the rule as it pleased them. Muldoon, Albert, and TJ were the beneficiaries of a dingo logic that required no rule to ever be written in stone.

The dingoes had also made an exception for Theodore and Bertram when they built the Gates of Hell. The building straddled the line between Hell and the rest of Old Australia, which created a certain territorial ambivalence in the dingoes. In addition, Theodore and Bertram would trade them guns for the coins and equipment they took from trespassers on the flats, and would give them the marsupials that had fallen victim to advertising and the killer possum. As TJ had pointed out, no intelligent animal ever passes up a gun or a free meal.

When Bertram had proven himself a coward at the fight at the water hole and Theodore had shown that he was willing to kill someone protected by a platypus, the dingoes knew that no good would come to them if they continued to associate with creatures that spineless or that reckless. They warned Bertram and Theodore never to return, and the pair had shunned the Gates of Hell ever since.

Albert shifted his position against the pack. His shoulder was still sore from the blow he had taken at Ponsby Station, and sitting in one position too long caused it to stiffen up. Jack had been quiet since they'd finished gathering firewood, and he had stayed in the shade of the acacia smoking his pipe and swatting flies.

When it began to get dark, Jack put some twigs on the coals under the tripod and brought the fire back to life.

"I tried to stop," he said suddenly.

"Tried to stop what?" Albert asked.

"Setting things on fire." Jack sat down under the bush and relit his pipe. "I thought that after what happened to Muldoon at Winslow, I'd never set another one."

He took a draw on his pipe. "But I was never sure. So I stayed away from towns as much as I could. I'd go in somewhere, sell a map or a rock I'd salted, get supplies, and get out. It worked for eight years."

"Ponsby Station." Albert was pretty sure what was coming next.

"And then we got to Ponsby Station and I burned the damned place down." Jack nodded sadly.

"Not all of it," Albert said thoughtfully.

"There is that, I suppose." Jack stopped talking and took in an occasional mouthful of smoke from his pipe.

"You set the fire to help me, Jack. You can't blame yourself for that." Albert was beginning to feel a little guilty that he had been responsible for Jack's relapse.

Jack shook his head. "Every fire I ever set, I set with good intentions. At least that's what I told myself. The problem is, Albert, if you like a thing too much, you can always find a reason for doing it. I might have been able to get Muldoon out of Winslow without setting fire to the hotel, and I might have been able to get you out of Ponsby Station without burning down O'Hanlin's place. But a fire was always the first thing that came into my mind, and once that happened I never considered trying anything else. If I had, there's a good chance Muldoon wouldn't have been killed and you wouldn't have a price on your head."

"Muldoon's not dead," Albert said quietly.

Jack didn't hear what Albert said, or if he did he ignored it.

"Muldoon wanted to fight in Winslow, but I was against it. Winslow was a tough town and a hard place to get out of if things went bad. But Muldoon was famous by then and felt his reputation was at stake. There was a pretty tough kangaroo in Winslow who had challenged Muldoon to a fight, no holds barred. The kangaroo had killed two opponents and was known as quite the wrestler in some parts of the territory. The locals thought highly of him . . . a little *too* highly, as it turned out.

"If Muldoon had let the fight go on for a while, we probably would have been all right. He knew how to string out a match. We had made a lot of money on side bets when we first started. He and I would do an exhibition match every so often and make it look like I came close to beating him. I couldn't beat him— nobody could—but we were pretty good at selling the illusion.

"Anyway, when Muldoon walked into the ring in Winslow and the crowd started booing him, I had a bad feeling. Muldoon hated being booed, and he hated having things thrown at him.

"The kangaroo was late in coming, and the longer Muldoon was in the ring by himself, the worse the crowd got. Pretty soon empty bottles and rotting vegetables started flying out of the crowd. Muldoon just stood there and didn't flinch even when he got hit.

"When the kangaroo finally showed, the crowd started to settle down. The kangaroo climbed into the ring and called

Muldoon a couple of names. Muldoon didn't say anything; he just walked over to the kangaroo and broke his neck. I'd never seen anything like that, and I know the crowd hadn't, either. It took them awhile to come after us."

Jack took another draw on his pipe, but it had gone out.

"We got back to the hotel ahead of the mob, but not by much. I set the place on fire to cover our run for the edge of town. The fire was going pretty good when Muldoon ran back inside."

Jack tapped his pipe on his knee for a few moments and then looked over at Albert. "It never crossed my mind that Muldoon would run back into the hotel, but it should have. I knew the medals were important to him, and I'd forgotten he'd left them in his room."

"Medals?"

Jack looked away from Albert and back toward the fire. "I didn't think they were much. But Muldoon set quite a store by them. He was never interested in the money we made. He'd buy sardines, and maybe a drink every so often, and not much else. But he liked medals, and he liked being carried on the shoulders of the crowd. He was the only one of his kind that ever got here, and I think the medals and the cheers made him feel a little less alone."

"What kind of medals were they?" Albert asked.

"What you'd expect. A piece of pot metal with a ribbon that said 'Champion' or 'Winner' or some such thing. Some local dignitary would hang one around his neck when he won a fight and tell him how great he was.

"I don't know if he believed what they told him—he didn't put much trust in others. But the medals were different; they were solid. He could carry them with him and hold them long after the crowds had disappeared."

Jack picked up a small stone at his feet and tossed it toward the fire. "At least, that's what I think now. We never really spoke again. But he had a partially melted medal in his paw when I pulled him out of the hotel."

"What happened after you got him out?"

Jack shrugged. "Not much else to tell. He was hurt a lot worse than I was, but I got him clear of the town and eventually got both of us back to our camp. I put him in his tent and nursed him as best I could. A few weeks later I went into a town to get supplies—and when I got back, both Muldoon and the tent were gone."

Jack got up slowly and looked out into the night beyond the camp.

"The Famous Muldoon died in that fire, and that was the only Muldoon I ever knew. A shadow is waiting for me out here, Albert. The shadow of a time long past, and I'm afraid of what I might find."

Before Albert could say anything, he heard what sounded like thunder coming from the distance. He stood up and walked over to where Jack was standing. The sky above them was clear, and the stars were bright as far as they could see.

There was a flash of light on the horizon, and a few seconds later another clap of thunder rolled over the camp.

27

Marsupials Forever

Albert left Jack at dawn, carrying nothing but a canteen, and walked the desert in the direction of the explosions he had seen light the sky the night before.

It was clear that things were happening on the flats of Hell that did not bode well for Albert and his friends. After what had happened at Ponsby Station, Albert was worried about leaving Jack alone. But it was clear that they needed information as quickly as they could get it, and he was the only one fit enough to act as a scout. He gave Jack the pistol and careful instructions: if a dingo showed up, Jack was to ask questions first and, if need be, shoot afterward.

Albert kept a brisk pace through the morning and came across a dingo encampment at noon. He searched through what remained of the camp, but he didn't find anyone still alive. The smell of black powder hung in the air, and brush shelters scattered around the small clearing were still smoldering. The midday sun had already dried the pools of blood around the bodies, and bush flies were everywhere in great numbers.

It hadn't been a big camp. Albert had counted only twelve bodies, mostly females and pups. It was hard to tell what had killed the dingoes—the bodies were badly torn, and all of them were missing their ears.

The camp had been built near a small spring, and the minute Albert approached it he could tell something was wrong. He might not know much about the desert, but he knew something about water.

There were footprints all around the spring, and none of them belonged to the bodies in the camp. Albert bent down and took a little of the water in one paw. It smelled of cities and had the color of tarnished copper. A few crayfish floated on the surface of the pool along with some dead insects. Whoever had killed the dingoes had also poisoned the spring.

Albert stood up and wiped his paw on the front of his jacket. Poisoning water was a crime of such enormity that he couldn't understand it. Water was where a platypus lived. It was the center of his being.

In some ways, he could understand the killing of other creatures. He had done it himself and could point to reasons, both good and bad, for having done so. He could find no reason in destroying that which was freely given to everyone. The spring was neutral. It had provided life for anyone that came to drink there, even to the ones who poisoned it. There had been no passion in its death, only a sad desire to kill the future.

He began to worry that some other passerby that didn't know water as well as he did might stop to drink there. He was looking for something to mark the spring when he heard another explosion in the distance.

The noise wasn't as far away as it had been the night before, and Albert thought he could get to the source in a fairly short time. What he would do when he got there depended on what he found.

He quickly made an arrow of rocks on the ground pointing to the spring and piled the dead crayfish at the point of the arrow. It wasn't much, but it was better than nothing. Albert took a last look at the spring and shook his head before jogging into the bush in the direction of the noise, which was continuing to repeat itself.

A mile from the dead dingoes Albert located the source of the explosions. A group of marsupials were entrenched around the base of a low hill that rose no more than twenty feet above the desert floor. On top of the hill a group of kangaroos were loading and firing a small cannon. A small figure was directing the gun crew, and every so often Albert could see flashes of light reflected from the goggles it was wearing.

Albert had never seen a cannon before, but this was obviously a big gun. It was firing large bullets into the bush somewhere beyond the hill.

Every time a shell exploded, the militia in the trenches would wave flags and cheer. Albert could hear faint cries of "Death to Dingoes" drifting in the wind from the hill, as well as the singing of a song that had "Marsupials Forever" as a chorus.

The hill gave those on top a good view of the surrounding desert, and Albert was afraid to get any closer than a thick stand of grevillea about half a mile from where the kangaroos were firing the gun.

He had been crouched in the bush for about twenty minutes when the firing stopped. He watched as the militia left the trenches and headed out into the bush toward where the shells had landed. Theodore and the gun crew stayed with the cannon.

A figure in a plumed hat climbed up the hill from the trenches and stood next to the gun. The figure took off its hat and waved it over its head. The cheering from the gun crew got louder. Albert thought the figure was probably Bertram, but it was difficult to be sure at that distance.

He turned to head back to where he had left Jack and almost ran into a dingo that had come up behind him. Startled, both Albert and the dingo jumped backward, but after the first moments of confusion things began to settle down.

The dingo was young, with just a few scars. Albert couldn't remember having seen him before, but he seemed to know Albert. The dingo pushed Albert back down behind the grevillea and watched the hill for a few minutes. When he was sure that their movements hadn't been seen, the dingo beckoned Albert to follow him and set off into the bush, keeping clumps of brush between them and the hill.

The young dingo led Albert away from the hill for some distance before angling back toward the militia trenches. They came to a shallow ravine and followed it to a small grove of acacia not very far from where Albert had watched the cannonade.

The early afternoon sun was filtering through the leaves of the trees, and the contrast between the light and small shadows made the center of the grove a study in two dimensions.

TJ was sitting on a log in the middle of the grove, surrounded by half a dozen silent dingoes. The dingoes raised their paws to the young one as it led Albert into the grove, and their salute was returned with the same quiet dignity.

TJ motioned to Albert to join him. He had on the clothes Albert had washed, and Albert could see a lump in his long johns where they covered the bandages. TJ looked very tired, but he smiled as Albert walked over to the log.

"Good to see you, partner."

"You, too, TJ."

The young dingo found a place among his kind and became one with the shadows of the grove.

"Sorry we couldn't get to you sooner. The dingoes didn't spot your tracks until a few hours ago. It's been kind of busy around here."

Albert sat down on the log next to TJ.

"That possum may be crazy, but he's not stupid, and that's for sure." TJ tipped his hat back and wiped his forehead with the back of his paw. "They've been bombarding a camp about a quarter mile from here. I think most of the dingoes got out before it started, but I'm not sure."

Albert took the canteen off his shoulder and offered it to TJ. "How are you doing?" he asked.

TJ shrugged and took the canteen. "I'm a little peaked yet. My lodge brothers over there had to half carry me out here." TJ gestured to the dingoes with the canteen. "I needed to know what we were up against, and I don't speak dingo real well." He took a drink from the canteen. "They keep those toy soldiers of theirs in groups and cover them with the cannon. Dingoes wouldn't have a chance going up against anything like that…It could be worse, I guess."

"What do you mean?" Albert asked as TJ handed back his canteen.

"They move real slow and have to set up the gun each time they come to a camp. The dingoes travel light and can keep away from them. I figure after a while they'll run out of food or get tired of chasing dingoes around Hell and head back to where they came from."

Albert shook his head. "It will be too late by then."

"Why?"

"They're poisoning the water."

TJ didn't say anything for a moment. Finally, he pulled his hat down. "Well, that puts the icing on the cake, doesn't it." He stood up. "Come on, boys, it's time to head back."

The dingoes moved out of the shadows, and one of them came over and stood next to TJ.

Albert jumped off the log. "TJ, we can't let them kill the springs."

TJ put his arm over the dingo's shoulder and leaned on him for support. "And we're not going to. It will be a cold day in hell before a damned possum and a one-eared rabbit outsmart Terrance James Walcott, and you can bet real money on it."

28

An Illusion of the Present

Jack had been exhausted when they reached Muldoon's camp. They had come a long way that day, and even with a guide it had been a hard trip. The young dingo, like most of his kind, wasn't used to dealing with cripples and didn't have much patience with Jack. Bad leg or not, he had to keep up.

Albert had carried Jack's pack for most of the day, but Jack was still a long way back when he walked into the center of the camp. TJ and a number of dingoes had already arrived, and there was a lot of activity going on around the water hole. Albert quickly took the packs he was carrying over to the edge of the water hole where he had slept before. He was heading back to collect Jack when Muldoon walked out of his tent.

At that moment, Jack stumbled out of the bush at the edge of the water hole, dragging his left foot and doing his best to keep upright. He and Muldoon saw each other at about the same time. After a moment's hesitation, Jack squared his shoulders and walked toward Muldoon, trying to disguise his limp.

Muldoon ducked back into his tent and came out with a canteen and two stools. He put the stools down by the tent entrance and waited for Jack with the canteen in his good paw. Muldoon made no move to help Jack, but let him make his way to the tent as best he could.

Jack reached the stools and sat down heavily. He looked up at Muldoon. "It's been awhile."

Muldoon gave the canteen to Jack. The cork was still in the canteen, and Jack and Muldoon had only two good paws between them. Jack held the canteen as Muldoon pulled out the cork with his good paw.

Jack took a drink. "Did I miss anything?"

Muldoon shook his head.

"That's good to know," Jack said as he gave the canteen back.

Albert walked away from Muldoon's tent and set up a place for him and Jack to sleep. He never again went near enough to hear what Muldoon and Jack said, but he watched them from time to time as he moved through the camp.

Jack's guilt had always been of his own making. If Muldoon had been hurt, he could blame only himself and the past events in his life that had driven him into the ring in Winslow. Albert was pretty sure they both understood this, but he couldn't be certain.

When Jack came back to Albert's camp later, he was too tired to say very much. Before he went to sleep, he told Albert that he was glad he'd come and that it had been important to both him and Muldoon.

Jack had been right when he said the Muldoon he knew had died in the hotel, but what he didn't say was that the Jack from those days was just as dead. The Jack that saved Albert was not the same creature who had limped into Muldoon's camp, and he would be a slightly different creature when he limped out.

Albert was beginning to believe that he might have died in the desert near the railroad, and that TJ might have died on the gangplank in San Francisco, and all they had before them was a chance to die another time in a different place. The coming morning might be the time, and the clearing he was sitting in could very well be the place.

The only lights in the desert that night came from Muldoon's camp and the fires of the militia on the rise a half mile away. Two days after Albert and Jack arrived at Muldoon's camp, TJ had sent word across the flats that no fires were to be lit in the dingo encampments beyond the water hole, and since that time there had been no other fires lit in Hell.

TJ had suspected it was the firelight that had drawn the militia, and he had been proven correct. The fires that had been left burning every night around Muldoon's tent had brought the militia to the water hole and, if the patterns of the past repeated themselves, the bombardment would begin just before dawn.

The glow of the fires and the light reflecting from the water, from the tent, and from the ragged canopy of the gum trees created a sense of theater in the camp that foreshadowed what was to come in the morning.

In a few hours, the dingoes were to let the fires die, and everyone in the camp except Albert would slip back into the bush beyond the range of the gun. TJ had said that if he had any choice he would have picked someone with longer legs, but Albert was the only chance they had.

In the last two attacks, after the initial bombardment, the militia had left the trenches they had dug and had gone into the deserted camps to poison the water and take trophies from the dead. There was no reason to believe they wouldn't do the same in the morning.

The militia needed to be given a reason to go far enough beyond their camp that the shells of the cannon couldn't protect them. TJ hoped that a short-legged platypus worth twenty pounds sterling dead or alive would be reason enough.

If he survived the bombardment, Albert was to wait in the camp until the militia spotted him, then run into the bush, making sure that Bertram's troops gave chase. The farther they chased him, the better. The militia had met no opposition so far, and they had likely become convinced of their invincibility.

TJ had originally considered using a few dingoes as bait— they were brave enough to do the job, and they could run a lot faster than Albert. But they looked pretty tough, and TJ was afraid the militia might have second thoughts about chasing them into the bush. He would hold them in reserve in case Albert was killed at the water hole.

Albert had dug a shallow burrow at the water's edge to use during the bombardment. He had taken the reward posters he had been saving and placed them on stunted trees between the water hole and the militia camp, just to make sure the coming marsupials knew that chasing a platypus could be a worthwhile endeavor. Albert had done all he could, and if it wasn't enough, he'd worry about it in another life.

He sat by himself in the middle of the camp. He would send his pack out with TJ and the dingoes when they left, keeping only his canteen. TJ wanted nothing left in the camp that the militia could use. He had asked Muldoon if he wanted to strike his tent and move it beyond the water hole and out of range of the cannon, but Muldoon just shook his head, and TJ let the matter rest.

TJ and some of the older dingoes were now gathered at one edge of the camp conversing in signs and monosyllables. Every so often young dingoes would come in from the darkness bringing information, then be sent back out again with a response from TJ or one of the elders.

Jack and Muldoon waited for word to leave the camp sitting under the canopy of Muldoon's tent. When they spoke, they spoke in low voices and Albert couldn't hear what they were saying.

He knew that eight years had passed since they had seen each other, and that those years had been hard on both of them. He thought there would be an awkwardness between them born of the pain they both carried from Winslow, but time had erased none of the familiarity they had shared so long ago. Albert watched as one or the other would cock his head or use a paw for emphasis, casting moving shadows on the wall of the tent.

The dingoes stopped feeding the fires, and one by one the lights around the water hole went out for the last time. Jack put on his pack and Muldoon came out of his tent wearing his pea-coat. He had made a bundle of his wrestling tights and was holding them under his good arm.

All that needed to be said had been said that afternoon, and with a brief wave Jack and Muldoon walked away. Two dingoes, one carrying Albert's pack and the other carrying TJ's carbine, helped TJ into the night. Albert was now alone in the deserted camp.

29

The Winners

The first shell sent up a geyser of water in the middle of the water hole, and the second hit Muldoon's tent. After that, Albert stopped paying attention. The morning air was dead still, and smoke from the explosions hung low on the ground. It wasn't long before Albert couldn't see more than a few feet from the edge of his burrow.

The shots came at measured intervals, and Albert had enough time between each explosion to consider his mortality. He began to wish that the intervals were shorter and gave him less time to think. All he could do was lie in the burrow, covered in pieces of yellow-and-red canvas, listening to each shell whistle as it dropped into the camp and hoping his luck would hold one more time.

As the morning passed, he became used to the noise of the cannon in the distance, the whistle and the detonation of the shells. Once or twice dirt had been thrown on him by shells that exploded close to his burrow, but he hadn't been hurt. Fatalism replaced fear as Albert realized it would take a direct hit to kill him.

He became more concerned with what was going to happen when the bombardment ended. The wind hadn't come up and the smoke had gotten thicker. If not for the water hole at his back, Albert would have no idea which way he was facing and where he expected the militia to enter the camp. Between explosions he tried to listen for movement, but all he could hear was the ringing in his ears.

It was quiet for a long time before Albert realized that the cannon fire had stopped. He stuck his head over the edge of his burrow and looked out into a gray haze. He could hear the faint sound of music in the distance beyond the smoke.

He crawled out of the hole he had dug and stood up. The music wasn't very good—it was just drums and bugles, one ragged, the other off-key, but it gave him some sense of the direction of oncoming militia. It wasn't long before he began to hear voices mixed with the beat of the drums.

He was going to have to start running pretty soon, but the militia would have to be able to see him first. The smoke wasn't something he or TJ had considered; it made everything more difficult and had lessened his chances of survival considerably.

Albert could smell the water behind him, and the instinct of untold generations of his kind told him that he would be safe there. He had learned the hard way that nothing was ever safe in Old Australia, but the urge to dive into the water hole was becoming stronger and stronger. Rather than risk a victory of instinct, Albert threw himself into the smoke and began running in the direction of the music.

He was only about ten yards from his burrow when he ran bill-first into a large kangaroo carrying a musket. They both jumped back in surprise.

"Platypus!" the kangaroo screamed.

Albert turned and was two steps back into the smoke when the kangaroo fired his musket. The shot missed, but it started a chain reaction. Guns began going off all around him. The air was full of the sounds of shots, screams of pain, and then more shots.

Albert had gone only a few more yards when he ran into a wallaby, armed to the teeth with rifle, pistol, and sword. The encounter scared the wallaby enough that he didn't have time to swing his sword before Albert disappeared again. He heard the wallaby yell, "There's another one over here!"

There were more shots, more yelling. Albert kept bouncing off marsupials as he ran through the smoke. He tried to keep running in a straight line, but each collision shifted his direction and produced more high-pitched yells of warning.

Gunfire rattled through the smoke and bullets were flying everywhere. Every so often, Albert would see a dim muzzle flash through the thick smoke and shift his direction to avoid the shooter.

Screams of "Platypus!" were coming from directions he'd never been, and with each scream, shooting throughout the camp intensified.

The cannon had started firing again, and Albert could hear the shells whistle overhead and explode somewhere beyond the camp. The sound of the gun gave Albert a vague sense of its location and he started running away from the noise.

He tripped over a dead bandicoot with a spear in it, and he lay in the dirt next to the body for a few moments. He could hear the yips of dingoes in the smoke around him and the thud of clubs mixed with pistol and rifle shots. The air was clearer close to the ground and Albert could see feet running past him, dingo feet and marsupial feet mixed together. Occasionally a body would drop out of the smoke near him to lie on the dirt whimpering or choking.

It was obvious that TJ's plan had unraveled and the fight was not happening beyond the range of the cannon. Albert's day as decoy was going badly, and he had no idea what he should do next. As he lay there, hoping for inspiration, the instinct that he had suppressed all morning began to reassert itself. The smell of water was very faint and was mixed with the stench of blood and black powder that surrounded him, but it was enough.

If he closed his eyes, Albert could sense where the water was. He began crawling forward. He opened his eyes every so often to make sure he wasn't crawling into someone being killed. If the way ahead of him was clear, he would close his eyes again and let his sense of smell guide him. The noise of the guns and the screams of the dying faded into idyllic scenes of the river of his childhood, and Albert began to crawl faster.

He could see his mother on the far bank, and he knew if he could reach her everything would be all right and he would be safe forever. He jumped up and started running. As he reached the bank of the river, he tripped over something and fell head-first into the water.

Albert opened his eyes and found himself in the water hole with his hat floating next to him. A cannon shell exploded over his head and blew shrapnel across the water in front of him. Albert grabbed his hat, shoved it in his vest, and dived under the surface.

He swam across the water hole, hugging the bottom the entire way. He surfaced on the far side and looked back toward Muldoon's camp. Except for a few patches of gray that floated above the water hole, the smoke stopped at the water's edge. He could see the body of the dingo that he had tripped over lying on the beach.

Fighting was still going on in the camp. He could hear shots and see muzzle flashes, but the shots were becoming less frequent. A slight breeze had come up and was starting to thin the smoke. Albert could see figures moving on the far side of the water hole and thought it prudent to move out of rifle-shot range before they could see him.

He climbed up on the bank and started jogging through the gum trees and into the hills on the far side of the water hole. Another cannon shell burst ahead of him and he could see smoke from the explosion. If he had any friends left, they probably had been the target, and he headed in that direction.

A hundred yards from the trees, he started coming across dead dingoes. They had been caught in the open, running toward the relative safety of the smoke-filled camp. They had been killed before they could strike a blow and, in dingo tradition, would remain unhonored where they lay. In time, the desert would reclaim the bodies.

Another shell flew overhead, and Albert saw where it landed. The shell hit in front of a large boulder, part of a rocky outcropping that had created another small hill on the desert floor. The minute the dirt from the explosion settled, TJ climbed onto the boulder and started waving his hat. The movement drew another shell, and TJ just managed to get off the boulder before it hit one of the other rocks. Stone fragments ricocheted off the face of the boulder. TJ climbed back up and started waving his hat again.

Albert heard the cannon go off, but there was no whistling and no shell fell. A minute later the cannon fired one more time and then there was silence.

TJ hesitated and then stopped waving his hat. He kept looking in the direction of the militia trenches. Finally, he sat down on the boulder and put his hat back on. Jack limped out from behind the rock where TJ was sitting. He had Muldoon's peacoat thrown over his shoulder and was carrying TJ's Enfield in his good paw. He leaned the rifle against the rock, sat down, and put Muldoon's jacket across his lap.

Albert worked his way through the bush to the rocks as quickly as he could. He stopped next to Jack, who looked up at him and gave him a sad smile but said nothing.

TJ was still breathing hard from climbing up and down the boulder. He looked down at Albert. "I wasn't sure I'd see you again."

Albert looked around. "Where's Muldoon?"

TJ waved a paw toward the militia trenches. "He's up there somewhere."

Albert looked out toward the water hole and the ridge beyond. He could see movement in the trees by the water hole, but the ridge was quiet.

"Did we win?" Albert asked.

TJ shrugged. "Wouldn't know. I've been stuck in this damn rock pile since the shooting started. It's been a hell of a fight, though."

Albert could feel the heat of the sun for the first time that day. He took his hat out of his vest and put it on. He heard a faint cry above him and looked into the sky. A crow flew over the rocks toward the far ridge. Albert watched the bird until it became too small to see anymore, then he looked over at TJ, who was struggling to get up.

"Give me a paw off this rock, would you, Albert?"

Albert saw a pile of stones behind the boulder, and he climbed up to TJ and helped him down. TJ leaned on him for a moment.

"I haven't seen a dingo since the shooting started at Muldoon's camp. When it sounded like you'd started a war down there, I couldn't hold them back. The cannon started up again, and that's when Muldoon took off. I tried to keep the gunners distracted, but I don't know if it helped much."

Albert looked over at Jack. The old wombat looked very tired, but managed another smile. "I told him I'd hold his coat, Albert. That's all anybody could ever do for Muldoon."

TJ took his paw from Albert's shoulder. "Who knows, we might have even won this damn thing." TJ held out his paw and helped Jack to his feet. "You head on out, Albert. Jack and I will be along directly."

"If it doesn't look good, you come back for us. A good run is always better than a bad fight, and I want you to remember that," TJ cautioned.

Albert nodded and walked quickly down the hill toward Muldoon's camp. He looked back once to make sure that Jack and TJ were moving, then made his way into the bush.

Another crow flew over his head and landed in the top of a gum tree near the water hole. It began to call out and Albert followed the sound. He reached one end of the water hole and saw a few dingoes moving through the dead that littered the ground where Muldoon used to live. More crows were gathering in the treetops, and they watched with unblinking interest as below them the dingoes gathered up the guns of the fallen.

Albert hurried on past the camp. He had seen enough death that it held no fascination for him. He knew there were other bodies waiting for him on the ridge, and that was bad enough.

Small parties of dingoes searched for any of the militia that might have survived. They seemed indifferent to him and passed him by without any acknowledgment.

He reached the base of the ridge and walked up into the abandoned militia positions. There were a few dead kangaroos and wallabies lying in the first trench, but dead dingoes littered the

208 • Howard L. Anderson

slope all the way up to the gun on the top of the ridge. Muldoon's body was lying in front of the gun emplacement just beyond the last trench.

Albert walked slowly up the ridge, avoiding the dead as best he could. He stopped a few feet from Muldoon. The last shot from the cannon had carried away Muldoon's bad arm, but the explosion that close to the muzzle had killed the gun crew. Theodore's body lay in back of the gun, partially covered by bloody kangaroos.

A light wind blew gently across the ridge and ruffled the fur that poked through the torn fabric of Muldoon's purple tights. He lay on his back with his head turned to the side and Albert couldn't see the burns on his face. Except for the terrible wound that had taken away his arm and shoulder, he looked every bit the Muldoon he once had been.

The dingoes that had charged the hill at his side were all dead. There was no one left alive who saw Muldoon's last fight. If there had been any cheers, Albert hadn't heard them. Muldoon had fallen with the quiet companions he'd had for the last eight years. In the end, he hadn't died alone.

Albert saw something shiny hanging around Muldoon's neck, but before he could bend down to look at it, he heard a hissing sound. Albert looked up into a set of goggles and the twin barrels of a shotgun.

Theodore was standing beside the cannon with his shotgun pointed at Albert. He started cackling, and foam began forming at the corners of his mouth.

"Zoo!" he whispered. Then he giggled and cocked the hammers of the gun.

"Zoo!" he screamed as saliva dribbled down the front of his uniform. He giggled again.

Albert heard the report of the rifle before he heard the sound of the bullet hum past his head. The minié ball caught Theodore in the chest and knocked him back against the gun carriage. The giggling stopped, and Theodore slid into the dirt beside the gun.

TJ took the Enfield off his shoulder and let Jack help him up the ridge. It took a long time for them to navigate the trenches and the dead, but they finally made it to Albert and Muldoon.

They stood silently together. TJ took off his hat and bowed his head for a moment. Jack bent down and put the jacket he was carrying under Muldoon's head. TJ put his hat back on.

"Anybody have a pistol?" he asked.

Jack reached in his coat pocket and took out the pepperbox. TJ traded the rifle for the pistol, went over to Theodore, and carefully shot him five more times.

Albert bent over and looked again at the shining object that had caught his attention. A misshapen disk hung around Muldoon's neck on an old string. Albert bent down and looked closer. The melted metal disk said "Winner," but some of the letters were hard to read.

Dingoes had come out of the bush and were moving up the ridge scattering red earth on those who had died trying to silence the gun. Albert hoped that wherever Muldoon had gone, the red pigment might mean more to him than the medal around his neck.

30

A Lesson in History

The Gates of Hell was dark except for one dim light that flickered through a dirty window in the back of the building. Albert waited until TJ positioned himself near the back door, then he walked around the building to the front entrance.

He carried Theodore's shotgun under his arm. TJ had given it to him after the fight at the water hole. Albert had never been a good shot, and TJ thought he might have better luck with a firearm that was more forgiving than a pistol.

It had been three months since Muldoon had died, and TJ was impatient to finish what Bertram had started when he had invaded Hell. Except for a plumed hat lying in one of the trenches, there had been no sign of the wallaby after the battle.

That day, there had been no talk of looking for Bertram. A sadness had settled over the water hole and had replaced, in most, the relief of still being alive. Even the dingoes were quieter than normal and were quick to scatter back across the desert without feast or celebration. They just walked away and left the dead, both friend and foe, to be eaten by the crows that had continued to gather in the trees.

TJ had put all he had into directing the fight, and he was content to let Albert gather their gear and help him walk far enough into the desert to where the sounds and smells of the water hole were a memory and not a reality.

Jack had stayed with Muldoon's body while Albert gathered the packs from the rocks beyond the water hole. Then he, too, left the battlefield for the last time and limped after Albert and TJ into a late afternoon on the flats of Hell.

They traveled slowly, not really caring where they went or how long it might take them to get there. When it became too dark to continue, they made camp where they found themselves, one place seeming to be as good as any other.

Albert made a fire, pulled blankets out of the packs, and passed them around. At the bottom of his pack he found the whiskey bottle he had given to Muldoon. He passed the bottle to Jack without comment. Jack took a drink and gave the bottle to TJ.

Albert sat down next to Jack and drank from his canteen. There seemed no need for conversation; they had acted out the parts given to them that day and their assignments for tomorrow could wait until the morning. One by one, they fell asleep.

At daybreak, they moved on in the same fashion as the day before, and so it went for two more days until they reached water. A small spring fed clear water into a small pool that overflowed into a stream lined with acacia and gum trees.

They stopped with an unspoken agreement that they had walked away from the recent past as far as they could, and it was time to live in the present and prepare for the future. The tasks they had done so many times before were done again with a certain relief in being able to escape into the familiar and the mundane.

Albert gathered firewood and hunted the water hole for crayfish. Jack searched the bushes for snakes, and when he was satisfied there were none he set up the tripod and made tea. TJ was still recovering from his wound, but he found the energy to wash his clothes and make sure that all the guns were loaded and in working order.

Over the weeks, a routine was established in the camp. Once the chores were done, they rested in the shade, swam in the water hole, and made conversation over tea and crayfish in the evenings. Several times, dingoes stopped by and would share their beetles and grubs in return for whatever TJ had roasted by the fire.

They never stayed long but would make signs to TJ, which he seemed to understand, then they'd leave as quietly as they had come. TJ said that the dingoes had saved the cannon for him, and as soon as their business with Bertram was sorted out, he was going to take the gun down to the coast. There was a chance the ship might show up again, and if it did, he was going to try to capture it and take up piracy. It was something he had never done before and he had an urge to give it a try.

Jack would smoke his pipe and tell stories about what happened to him or to Muldoon long ago in the small-minded towns that were scattered throughout Old Australia. He would often get confused and repeat the same story several times. TJ and Albert always pretended they were hearing it for the first time.

Muldoon was always there in Jack's stories, but it was the Muldoon from before the fight in Winslow. They were always young in the stories, with Muldoon's fame still ahead of them. In those days, each new town was just another adventure and not a tragedy waiting to happen.

Albert listened to TJ and Jack in the evenings, but he never told any stories of his own. His days in Adelaide were all he could have spoken about, but they were dark days, best left as fading memories. He hoped that someday he would be able to sit with new friends and relate to them the things that he had seen and done in Old Australia. But that hope lay in an uncertain future, and for now he was content to listen to familiar voices tell tales about places he'd never seen.

As TJ's wound healed, he became restless. At first he would take short walks up the stream, stopping to rest in the shade of the trees. The walks became longer and the rests less frequent. Soon, he began taking his rifle and disappearing into the desert for hours at a time. One day, after being gone from before sunrise until after dark, he came back into camp and told Albert and Jack that the time had come to return to the Gates of Hell.

The dingoes had reported that they had seen some lights coming from the building and there was a good chance that Bertram had returned. Even if Bertram wasn't there, they could destroy his printing press and burn the building.

It took them four days to reach the Gates of Hell. Jack was still dragging his left leg, and it slowed the march considerably. No matter how long it might take them to get to their destination, there had been no question about leaving Jack behind. He had been responsible for rescuing Albert in Barton Springs and had been under fire at the water hole. He had a right to be there when the Gates of Hell met its end.

Albert was pretty sure that Jack didn't hold Bertram responsible for Muldoon's death and in some ways might have been grateful to him for indirectly providing the relief that Muldoon had been looking for. But he knew if there was going to be a fire, Jack wouldn't want to miss it.

A large militia recruiting poster covered the sign by the door, but other than that, the front of the Gates of Hell looked much as Albert remembered it. The wind had shredded the corners of the poster, and the glue holding it to the sign was beginning to give way.

Albert shifted the shotgun to his right paw and pushed the door partway open with his left. He listened for a moment and heard a faint scratching noise coming from inside the building. He slipped into the Gates of Hell through the half-opened door.

Bertram was sitting at the table in the center of the room. He was wearing a uniform jacket covered with gold braid and writing on a sheet of foolscap with a steel pen. A pile of papers sat on the table next to a candle and a full shot glass. There wasn't a tablecloth on the table, and the noise of pen on paper was clearly audible in the quiet of the room.

Bertram looked up briefly as Albert came in the door. "For a moment, I thought it might be Theodore."

"I wouldn't wait up for him, if I were you." Albert looked across the room and saw TJ standing in the darkness at the back of the room. The Enfield was cradled in his arms.

"I suspected as much. He was a brave and noble creature. I'll miss him." Bertram looked down at the paper and started to write again. "It's all in here. Theodore's valiant stand. His tragic end. How we saved Old Australia from the dingoes and their accomplices. In addition, I have included a section about how I rose from humble origins to the rank of General in the Armies of Old Australia. I'm hoping it will be an inspiration to others."

"I hope you're close to the end," TJ said very quietly.

Bertram looked over at TJ and shrugged. "I've already written the part where I am betrayed for the last time and murdered in cold blood by a foreigner and a platypus." He put down his pen and took a drink. "You will be long forgotten, while my name will still be on every lip. A martyr to the preservation of the marsupial way of life. There will be a statue of me in every square."

TJ tipped his hat off the back of his head and let it hang from his neck by the chinstrap. He scratched an ear. "I never thought of that," he said.

Bertram smiled. "That's because you lack my imagination."

TJ kept scratching his ear. "Maybe we ought to let you go. What do you think, Albert?"

Albert was confused. He didn't want Bertram to escape, but he didn't like the idea of killing him in cold blood. "I don't know, TJ. He tried to kill us."

Bertram continued to smile. He took the sheet of paper he'd been writing on and placed it carefully on top of the manuscript. He folded the manuscript and put it in his jacket pocket.

"I know he did, Albert, but he wasn't very good at it," TJ said. "I look at it this way. As a constable, Bertram here got an entire town burned down. As a general, he got an army wiped out. If we let him go, he will get elected to public office, and inside of a week there won't be a live marsupial left in Old Australia." He started laughing.

For the first time Bertram became visibly angry. "Do you think all that matters?" He stood up and reached back in his pocket and took out the manuscript. He shook it at TJ. "This is what matters. History is what matters."

TJ took the rifle out of the crook of his arm. "You talk too much, Bertram. Get out of here before I change my mind."

Bertram reached over and picked up the shot glass. He finished his drink and tossed the glass into the corner of the room.

Then he started toward the front door, but he looked at Albert and hesitated. He spun on his heel and pushed past TJ.

"I still don't believe in demons," he muttered to himself as he stepped out the back door and slammed it behind him.

TJ started poking around the piles of junk that cluttered the back of the room. "Might be something we can use in here. Help me look."

Albert slung the shotgun over his shoulder and went over to where TJ was. "Are you sure it was a good idea to let Bertram go?"

TJ smiled. "Don't worry, Albert. If he'd gone in your direction, I would have shot him before he got out the door. As it is, we've got friends out back."

Albert and TJ searched through the piles of furniture, stacks of barrels, and crates that surrounded the printing press standing along the back wall. They were still looking when Jack came in the back door. He waved to them and then he, too, began rummaging around at the back of the store.

Most of the barrels and boxes were empty, and the bolts of cloth moth-eaten. TJ found a couple of bars of lead and put them in a pocket. Albert was hoping to find his old rucksack that he had lost the first time he'd come to the Gates of Hell. He was sure the money that had been stolen was long gone, but he missed the rucksack.

Albert moved a dusty crate that had once contained parts for the printing press. Behind the crate something shiny reflected the light from the lone candle in the room. He bent down and took a closer look. The soft drink bottle he had brought from Adelaide was lying on the floor.

He picked up the bottle and wiped the dust off it with the

sleeve of his coat. He had forgotten about the bottle. He didn't need it anymore, but it was all he had left from his days in Adelaide. As he put the bottle in the pocket of his coat, he smelled paraffin.

Jack was limping around the interior of the building carrying a large tin of lamp oil. He was pouring it on anything that looked flammable. When the tin was empty he threw it toward the front door and went looking for another one. TJ ran over and grabbed the candle off the table before the fumes could reach it and carried it to the back door. Albert edged closer to the door and waited until Jack poured a second tin of paraffin all over the floor.

"I never had this much time before," Jack said. "It sort of takes the fun out of it."

TJ carefully opened the back door before he gave Jack the candle. "If you're not careful, there's liable to be more fun than you had in mind." He jumped out the back door with Albert close behind him. They were fifty feet from the building when they heard the paraffin ignite. They turned to see Jack silhouetted in the doorway and flames pouring from every window of the building. Jack took a long look into the fire before he limped back to where Albert and TJ were standing. He hauled himself a few feet farther and sat down on the desert floor, facing the fire. TJ and Albert sat in the dirt next to him.

The fire engulfed the Gates of Hell in a matter of minutes, and the shingles on the roof began to glow. Inside the building, the fire reached the store of signal rockets and they began going off. Some flew skyward through the burning shingles; others shot through windows and burning siding to skitter along the ground and explode somewhere in the darkness of Hell or to shoot into the boulder field and ricochet into the night of Old Australia.

Flaming debris from the Gates of Hell blew into the sky, and the wind carried it across the desert as far as they could see.

Not far in the distance, Albert could hear the dingoes eating Bertram. The noise didn't bother him as much as it did when he had heard them eating O'Hanlin. But then, Albert had never cared much for Bertram.

31

The Distant Mountain

Albert watched TJ and the two dingoes climb a low hill not far from where they had parted company. If it wasn't for the blue bandana TJ had tied around his head, Albert would have had difficulty telling him apart from his companions.

They had left the last encampment at daybreak. Two young dingoes had come with them—not for any real purpose, just for something to do. The day was cool and the walking was easy. The mountain was still there on the horizon, seeming no closer than it had ever been. Before the sun was very high in the morning sky they came to the edge of Hell and the dingoes would go no farther. There were no markers on the desert floor to indicate that one patch of ground was different from another one a few feet away, but the dingoes knew that this was where their world ended.

The three old friends had stood on the edge of a new world and said good-bye to each other for the last time. In turn, TJ shook Jack's and Albert's paws.

"You boys take care of yourselves, and if you ever meet anybody else from California, you buy them a drink with the compliments of Terrance James Walcott."

"We'll do that," Jack replied.

TJ smiled.

"Well, Albert, we can't say it hasn't been interesting, can we?"

"No we can't, TJ, and that's for sure," Albert said. "Good luck in the piracy business."

"And good luck to you, my friend."

TJ turned and began jogging back the way they had come. The two young dingoes followed him and they soon disappeared into the bush, only to appear for a moment on the distant hill.

There had been some talk of staying together, but Albert knew that he wouldn't make a very good pirate, and there was not much chance that TJ would enjoy living anywhere shootings weren't a daily occurrence.

TJ had tried to talk Jack into going with him to capture the mystery ship. He told Jack that his limp might prove to be an advantage in the piracy business. TJ had heard that some of the best pirates had wooden legs, and a bad limp was just one step below having a peg.

Jack had thanked TJ for the offer but said that he was a little old for hopping around a deck trying to hit someone with a cutlass—and any day now he would go back to someplace beyond the lava field and take up prospecting again.

Albert knew he had no choice but to continue the journey he had started so long ago. He would walk toward the mountain that had been his guide ever since he had first left Ponsby Station. If Muldoon had been right and everyone who walked far enough ended up in Old Australia, there was a chance that walking even farther might take him to the place he was really looking for. The dingoes had let TJ know that Hell stopped long before it reached the mountain. If so, there might be another platypus out there somewhere the dingoes had never been.

Albert had asked Jack if he would like to come with him to the mountain. He knew that Jack's prospecting days were over and that leaving the old wombat alone with the dingoes wasn't a good idea. Jack's pride kept him from accepting Albert's offer for a few days, but he finally let himself be talked into going.

Jack and Albert made quite a show of deciding what to take with them and what not to take. In reality, all the things they owned amounted to very little, and they could have left an hour after deciding to go. But they needed to adjust to the idea of never seeing TJ again, and the time they spent packing helped make them feel a little bit better about leaving.

TJ stopped on the crest of the hill for a moment and looked back toward Albert. He raised his paw in the fashion of the dingoes. Albert did the same. TJ disappeared for the last time, and Albert turned back toward the mountain. Jack and Albert walked through midday, stopping often to let Jack rest. The land around them was changing slightly. The dirt was more rust colored, rocky outcroppings were becoming more frequent, and acacia was giving way to stunted trees. Jack took no interest in his new surroundings, but now and then would look back in the direction of Muldoon's last fight.

A few hours before sunset, Jack told Albert he couldn't go any farther. Albert dropped his pack and helped Jack off with his. He put the packs on the ground and half carried Jack to the shelter of some rocks a few hundred yards ahead of them.

When Albert returned to the rocks with the packs, Jack was slumped against a large stone. He had tried to light his pipe but the effort had been too much for him. He sat there with his pipe in one paw and a box of matches in the other.

Albert took the pipe and matches and put them on the ground

next to Jack. He took a blanket out of his pack and put it around Jack's shoulders. Jack thanked him and said he'd be ready to go in just a little bit. Then he closed his eyes and went to sleep.

Above Jack's head, Albert saw the picture of an animal carved in the stone. He looked at it closely, but windblown sand had eroded the picture and he couldn't tell what kind of animal it was. Albert looked around him and saw that the carvings were everywhere: stick figures of men, outlines of kangaroos, bandicoots, dingoes, wombats, and hundreds of other animals, some he knew and others he'd never seen before.

Albert walked around all the rocks and looked carefully, but he couldn't find a picture of a platypus. There was a chance that there had been a drawing of one and the wind had taken it away.

He sat down where he could keep an eye on Jack and see the mountain ahead of him. Even if no other platypuses had passed this way, the place he had dreamed of finding when he left the zoo was still ahead of him. He was sure that someday he would get there.

He had walked into Old Australia with an empty bottle, and he would walk out having learned about fame and friendship. He hadn't come from Adelaide to look for those things, but he had found them. He hadn't discovered why he had come to the place he was leaving, and he probably never would. The why of things had ceased to trouble him, and he was content with what he'd been given. The soft drink bottle from the zoo was still in his pack, and he would carry it to the distant mountain along with all the things he had learned on the flats of Hell.

The late afternoon sun lit the desert in front of Albert in a way he had never seen before. Piles of rocks floated in a bloodred sea of sand. Clumps of saltbush danced for him all the way to the mountain. Albert sat there in the beauty of that afternoon, glad to have Jack there with him, and grateful for days yet to come.

After the desert disappeared in the darkness, Albert walked over to adjust Jack's blanket against the chill of the night and found that Jack was dead. He adjusted the blanket anyway. Then he sat down next to the body and stayed there through the night, speaking to Jack about the life in Adelaide that had meant so little to him, as well as about all the things that he, Jack, and TJ had done together that had meant so much. By the time the sun came up there was nothing left to say.

Albert laid Jack on a blanket where he would be able to see the light of every morning and any star that fell in the night sky. He placed Jack's pack under his head and covered him with his old drover's coat. Then he put a can of sardines next to him, hoping he'd get a chance to share it with Muldoon somewhere down the line.

Albert packed his gear, put on his hat against the morning sun, and started walking into the desert toward the mountain on the horizon. Behind him, he could hear the stones begin to cry.

About the Author

HOWARD L. ANDERSON has had a varied life: he flew with a helicopter battalion in Vietnam and worked on fishing boats in Alaska, in the steel mills of Pittsburgh, as a truck driver in Houston, and as a scriptwriter in Hollywood. After earning a law degree, he became legal counsel for the New Mexico Organized Crime Commission. He is currently a defense attorney in New Mexico, where he represents people from Mexico charged with crimes north of the border.

Reading Group Guide

Discussion Questions

1. In the preface to ALBERT OF ADELAIDE, Howard L. Anderson writes, "As with most stories, hope rather than truth wins out with each telling." Do you agree or disagree with this assertion? How does the novel illuminate this idea?

2. When he encounters Jack the wombat, Albert is made aware of his nakedness for the first time. How is Albert changed when he acquires clothes? Does this mark a shift in the nature of his journey?

3. The animals Albert encounters in Old Australia are far more humanlike—though not necessarily more civilized—than those he lived among at the Adelaide Zoo. What accounts for this difference?

4. "At the zoo, Albert had been an object of curiosity and ridicule. In Old Australia, he found himself an object of hate and mistrust," writes Anderson. For Albert, his journey to Old Australia holds the promise of finding others like him, but upon arriving there, he is disappointed by what he discovers. What about being around people similar to us fosters confidence and a sense of security?

5. Are the differences among animal species in ALBERT OF ADELAIDE comparable to the differences among human

races? Ethnicities? Nationalities? Or is it a subtler or more pronounced distinction?

6. Is there a hierarchy in Old Australia—among wombats, wallabies, possums, bandicoots, kangaroos, dingoes, and Tasmanian devils? If so, is it a fixed hierarchy or does it evolve over the course of the novel? How does Albert fit into the order of things?

7. Albert is searching for Old Australia but quickly discovers that the place he imagines no longer exists—or perhaps never did. What have you discovered while searching for something else?

8. In ALBERT OF ADELAIDE, it's not always clear who is the hero and who is the villain. Is there an absolute code of ethics in Old Australia? If so, what is it?

9. What are Albert's core convictions? What are Jack's? How does Albert learn to adapt to a world with morals that are at odds with his own? When have you had to bend your convictions to conform to those around you?

10. A wild frontier setting and the dramas that arise from living there are elements common to most traditional westerns. How does ALBERT OF ADELAIDE both conform to and satirize this convention?

11. Howard L. Anderson's novel uses the elements of many literary genres—the traditional western, the fantasy, and the buddy novel. What aspects did he choose from each and why? How do they interact to form something new?

12. At the close of the book, where do you think Albert is heading? Do you think it will it be worth leaving the only friends he's ever known?